T0115050

A Town Untangled

Mystery, History, and Mayhem

D. S. Sully

iUniverse, Inc.
New York   Bloomington

A Town Untangled

iUniverse books may be ordered through booksellers or by contacting:

iUniverse
1663 Liberty Drive
Bloomington, IN 47403
www.iuniverse.com
1-800-Authors (1-800-288-4677)

Because of the dynamic nature of the Internet, any Web addresses or links contained in this book may have changed since publication and may no longer be valid.

ISBN: 978-1-4401-9079-7 (sc)
ISBN: 978-1-4401-9081-0 (dj)
ISBN: 978-1-4401-9080-3 (ebk)

Library of Congress Control Number: 2009912228

Printed in the United States of America

iUniverse rev. date: 3/8/2010

Contents

Acknowledgments

A Town Untangled is dedicated to my father, Robert, whose tales of El Squeeko and postcard collection turned me into a storyteller as well.

Special thanks to David Schuh, whose skills as a wily computer wizard made this endeavor technically possible.

Foreword

Not long ago, or far away, I began untangling the antics and ancestry of my hometown. In doing so, a rediscovery brought me to the point where I first ventured from young whippersnapper toward eventual old coot. As this endeavor intensified, a landslide of surprises and suppressed memories rumbled forth. Unbeknownst to me, entwined myths, traditions, and mysteries were about to be untangled.

After considerable reflection, a relentless inquisition ensued. Both willing and reluctant informants were methodically interrogated to ascertain the gospel truth about the stomping grounds of my youth. Were the down-home characters I remembered really that quirky? Did my recollections of odd events actually occur? How truly peculiar was this place? To find the answers, steps needed to be retraced.

As this mission persisted, it was never my intent to become the town crier or a tattler of tales. Nonetheless, the result has been a revelation of the influences bestowed by ragamuffins and rabble-rousers, young twits and old maids, blabbermouths and silent types, spiritual mentors and enlightening spirits, and of course, wisecrackers and numbskulls. Just where this scribe fits in is up for grabs.

Maybe we have something in common. There's a possibility that eccentric elders, spooky neighbors, and mysterious others existed where you grew up. Perhaps reclusive cemeteries, moonshiners, and brothels remained discreet while overindulged citizens, oversized cops, and overzealous teachers got plenty of attention. And for sure, at least one local residence served as a sideshow salvaged yard.

Because of all this, I now know that a hometown is much more than just personal encounters and remembrances. Once exposed, however, any twisted roots thus associated must be delicately unraveled. After reading the transcribed banter of these explorations, you may also be compelled to untangle the past of your own hometown and then realize without a doubt, there really is no place like home. So be it.

Beastly
Mansion

Once upon a town untangled, a hideous dweller of the cellar, an imposing spirit hound, and a hidden passageway resided within a vintage mansion. Although concealed from most others, the presence of each was forever made known to me. Inside this enchanted dwelling, its expansive nineteen rooms, six entryways, four staircases, dual attics, and a chambered basement created a maze of mystery. The enormous ironclad pantry vault and rare grand piano, both orphaned by their deceased owner, added even more intrigue to such an archaic house of curiosities and calamities. As an eccentric elder, freakish groans and belches echoed through its twisted arteries of brass pipes and radiators. At times, even the walls trembled. Perhaps it was haunted, perhaps possessed; to me, it was simply home.

This Victorian aristocrat was adorned with interior Gothic columns, stained glass windows, beveled glass French doors, crystal chandeliers, and a marble fireplace. Its gabled roof wore a fedora of ornate slate tiles. The entryway cupola donned a matching tile top hat. Crowned by carved balusters and railings, the pillared porches framed the east and north sides. Shuttered and trimmed with handcrafted headers, the windows were festooned in fairy-tale fashion. As an antiquated abode on the village main street, it was nothing more and nothing less than just a big ol' house in a tiny ol' town of poorly kept secrets.

Located across the street from the home of grampy Sully, the mansion had past ties to our Irish relatives. It was built in the early twentieth century for a wealthy merchant from Great Britain, who later added to his riches by becoming the town's grocery baron. The land on which this stately house had been constructed once belonged to my Gaelic great grandfather Jerry, the township blacksmith, who died at the age of thirty-two when kicked in the chest by a surly draft horse. The smithy had originally deeded the lot to the English storekeeper with the stipulation that it would revert back to Irish ownership in the absence of heirs. This British immigrant, named Charles, and his two sisters who resided with him had no children. As such, the Englishman owned the house

D. S. Sully

while the Irishman claimed the land. The forgotten and later resurrected property covenant led to the purchase of the mansion by my father, Robert. Initially, the mansion commanded far too high a price to procure. Upon Grampy Sully's intervention and reference to the Celtic covenant, the British residence suddenly became affordable for acquisition by my family.

In times past, this mansion had been an elegant establishment. Well into its golden years when acquired by my family, it now desperately needed physical therapy. Mother Nature took her toll by peeling the paint, rotting the porch pillars, and weathering the roof. The plastered interior walls and ceilings bore roadmaps from years of foundation settling. The temperamental exterior doors changed seasonally by swelling shut during humid summers and shrinking throughout winter. Due to sparse insulation, massive icicles formed along the roofline and hung like stalactites until the spring thaw. Adding a bit of whimsy, these frozen formations became the imaginary crystal fangs of polar dragons and gnarly fingers of ice trolls attempting to gnaw and claw their way out of attic internment. This frigid fantasy was shared by the windows as well. The drafty nature of their single-pane construction resulted in an indoor accumulation of frost that often served as glass canvases for fingertip artwork on subzero days. Well marked by pathways of worn varnish, the creaking hardwood floors seemed tuned by decades of meandering footsteps. To say the least, this house had more than its share of body language.

In addition to the traditional top floor attic, an obscure chamber lay secluded at the back of the second floor. Accessed by its own stairway, this area consisted of an upper level cavern complete with cobwebs and dark places. A small dormer window allowed just enough light to compose shadows. The slanted walls, unfinished floorboards, and exposed chimney that jutted through the midsection further enhanced its foreboding feel.

The four upstairs bedrooms of this mansion became a matter of sibling hierarchy. My younger brother Tom and I shared the smallest bedroom. As the youngest, Scott occupied a corner space

4

in our parents' adjacent room. Graced by French doors and bay windows, the most elegant sleeping quarters belonged to my sister Kathy. Down the hallway, eldest brother Jim commanded a spacious three-room suite. His front room served as a body shop and salvage yard for plastic scale-model cars and trucks. The adjoining small storeroom was stacked with comic book and baseball card collections. The back room, where he slept, had a less wholesome distinction. Next to Jim's bed was an exit door leading to a cloistered flight of steps that separated him from an eerie attic. Any sounds echoing within this corridor or the storeroom also reverberated in his bedroom. As a safeguard against all things unknown, an inside bracketed two-by-four barricaded Jim's back door from any outside entry.

At the west end of this property loitered a four-room vintage carriage house that never quite adapted to becoming a garage. Wrinkled and gray on the outside, its geezer status became even more apparent by a dilapidated interior of wooden floors that cascaded from decades of sagging and warping. Left over in one room was the remaining woodpile from an era when a wood-burning stove commanded the mansion's kitchen. Another room, at the southeast corner, resembled a horse stall. Directly above it rested a loft inhabited by varying remnants of crown molding, wainscoting, balusters, and railings. Unlit and outmoded, this neglected fogy now served primarily as a make-believe fortress during neighborhood war games. An attached outside ladder added to these playtime endeavors by allowing rooftop surveillance from an imaginary watchtower. In doing so, this old timer maintained a legacy of horsing around.

Less than forty feet away stood a wooden storage building that was much older and smaller than the carriage house. It belonged to a grandmotherly widow named Frita. What rested within revealed its true character. One late summer day, a pilot named Barney buzzed over the neighborhood and landed his red airplane in a nearby field. The plane was quickly shuttled down to this shed. After dismantling the wings, the entire assemblage became imprisoned inside. Local kids, who knew of this curiosity, took advantage of newcomers by betting them that a real airplane could fit into the miniscule shack. I would almost wager that it is still there. Before evolving into an aeronautical tomb, this shack served as the base station where Frita's grandsons, Rod and Jeff, built go-carts from wood scraps, metal parts, and discarded lawnmower engines. Leaning against this shed was also the high-rise bike they invented by turning the frame upside down and extending both the seat and handlebars to six feet above ground level. Available to any neighborhood daredevil, either a ladder or nearby tree was needed to mount this contraption. Dismounting was left up to your own ingenuity.

Frita's modest property also included an old stone wall that encased an enormous culvert. The traditional initiation into adolescence required venturing deep into this galvanized gully and remaining among the cobwebs until an 18-wheeler thundered overhead.

Sheltered between the carriage house and a grove of lilacs stood the venerable outhouse. Following the property's purchase, this sanctuary experienced a momentous demise. During an outdoor auction of the mansion's furnishings, a sizeable crowd had gathered. Due to the decaying condition of the outhouse, signs were posted to prevent any occupancy. Unfortunately for one auction attendee, an incorrigible sense of urgency could not be contained. Retreating to the outhouse and ignoring the warnings, he opened the door and entered. Moments later, resonating sounds of collapsing timbers and frantic screams brought the auction to a standstill. The crowd gawked in amazement as several plucky rescuers began retrieving the ill-fated soul from the depths below. The following day, this regrettable refuge from the past was filled in and sealed off forever.

Although one perilous pitfall had been eliminated, it did not take long to detect that further dangers lurked inside the mansion. While exploring the house, we discovered a secret passageway in the back of the front foyer closet. Concealed beneath the main stairway was an unlit corridor of steps leading to the musty depths of the basement and the most diabolical of demons. A bizarre monster with huge appendages thrust into the ceiling resided in our creepy cellar. It was unclear whether the monster was about to lift the house off its foundation or drag it down into the abyss from which it came. Either way, the monster held our homestead hostage. Its rigor mortis nature fooled no one. Morbidly faceless, except for steely lips and toothless jaws, the dweller was, for the most part, mindless as well.

During the summer months, this pale creature of asbestos-laced and blemished skin hibernated. As winter approached, it slowly awakened and demanded to be spoon-fed carbon candy by the shovelful. Like an ancient dragon, the embers smoldering deep within its belly belched an earthen and oily breath. To extract undigested wastes called clinkers, my father routinely poked a long iron rod with claws on one end into the beast's glowing gut. Whatever rituals it commanded, my father obeyed. This included monitoring an intricate life support system of tubes, valves, and gauges.

Within the basement, a vast pantry served to nourish the beast. Truckloads of the black nuggets on which it fed were poured through an outside window until the pantry was filled to capacity. Next to this storeroom was a dank chamber with a dirt floor. During my first underworld expedition, I saw what appeared to be bones in the far corner of this secluded root cellar. Not immune to an adolescent imagination and suspicious of all things dark and dreary, I avoided the secret passageway for years.

This was easily achieved, as there were three other stairways within the house. One served as the primary entrance to the basement while the other served the upstairs. These upper levels, however, offered no haven from the heavy breathing behemoth in the bowels of this dwelling. Its steamy breath and perspiration blasted through every brass radiator and pipeline. On the coldest of winter days, the sheer force of the beast's groans seemed destined to burst its overheated arteries. Eventually, I outgrew my fear of this monster, yet I never grew to like it.

Along with the cellar dweller, other creatures inhabited this property. In the lofty pines bordering the north lawn, a colony of screech owls took up residence. Their nightly chorus contributed to an eerie ambiance. So did the bats that shared these trees and flew wildly about on summer evenings. On occasion, an errant winged rodent would dart into the house and be repelled by the swinging of a tennis racket or broom. A giant box elder tree guarded the rear flank of the house, which led to a fall invasion of creepy crawlers. On one occasion, my brother captured a box elder bug and secretly placed it in my glass of chocolate milk. To this day, I wince before downing any such drink.

Our home was taller than the surrounding homes, which made the mansion serve well as the main residence for roosting pigeons. The obnoxious cooing became a routine wake-up call. A neighborhood kid decided to eradicate the problem by showing off his archery skills. Through sheer luck, rather than precision marksmanship, the young archer managed to nail a pigeon on his first shot. The arrow lodged just under the bird's skin without mortally wounding it. For days, the defiant feather-brain perched outside our upstairs bathroom window while showcasing a protruding shaft. Eventually, the arrow-clad critter flew away.

However, our neighborly bow hunter, who would someday become a town cop, continued with his boyhood escapades. During a backyard winter hunt, he took aim at a cottontail. Caught by the wind, the arrow was quickly out of control and sailed into an adjacent yard where two brothers were building a snowman. As the arrow scraped across Pat's shoulder, his brother Mike dashed into their house screaming that Indians were attacking. A year later, a different young neighbor accidently shot his brother in the left eye while testing his homemade bow and arrow. Needless to say, playing cowboys and Indians in this neighborhood required cautious consideration.

Fortunately, there was a means within our mansion to drown out all the external clamor of critters and calamities. An exquisite grand piano had been left behind by its original owner. Imported from England, it was one of four exclusive creations by its European artisans. Positioned on a floor reinforced with sturdy timbers, the incomparable and eloquent instrument dwarfed everything around it. Occupying a quarter of the spacious parlor, it was far more than just a mere music maker. It was difficult for my brothers, sister, and me to truly appreciate the majesty of such a grandiose piano. However, we cherished it as the perfect fort and hiding place. With blankets hung loosely about it, the space beneath this ebony titan quickly converted to a secretive clubhouse. Rather than the traditional three-legged cutaway design, this grand piano's unique shape was rectangular. Its four ornately carved legs were massive enough to obscure participants during a game of hide and seek. There were also times when the ivories were tunefully stroked by my mother and sister. Deserving of a magnificent stage setting, nonetheless, this musical masterpiece was cherished as both a fine instrument and a citadel of our playful imaginations.

At the very back of the mansion was what can only be described as an oddball room. With a dirt surface beneath its wooden floor and wainscoted walls, it obviously had been added on as a makeshift mud room. Elevated about two and one-half feet off the ground, there were no steps leading to its backdoor entrance. To enter or exit, one simply jumped up or down. This room had a partition dividing it into two separate areas. One side housed an abandoned ringer washer. The other half, with its sliding door and elevated entryway, became the perfect doghouse for Cookie. The name of Cookie was not of our choosing for this pedigreed pooch. It was bestowed on him as a pup, and now that he had moved in with us during his twilight years, it was too late for a change. As a regal, pure-white German shepherd with a wolf-like facade, he deserved better in terms of christening. I always thought that White Fang, Rex, Duke, or King would have been more suitable, yet the original name stuck. Aging and severely arthritic, this weary watchdog had become a "crumbling Cookie." He spent most days convalescing in the back yard. Occasionally, Cookie would resurrect enough energy to play with his favorite toy, an old metal hubcap chewed beyond recognition. In the midst of his golden age, Cookie's reign as a fearsome guard dog was all but past. There would be, however, a final curtain call to showcase his eminence.

As a house with quaint character, the old mansion always received its share of attention from the Halloween masqueraders. Sometimes a neighborhood window or two got soaped on this spookiest of nights. Usually this was only a minor irritation. There came a time, however, when my older brother Jim had just obtained a classic '57 Chevy. Newly painted in metallic apple green, it was parked on the south side of our lawn. Jim agonized over the prospect of his customized coupe being soaped. For security, Jim called upon Cookie to uphold the noble legacy of this guard dog breed. Barely able to amble about or muster a menacing howl, Cookie was of little threat to anyone. However, appearances can be deceiving. Chained to the chassis of my brother's car, Cookie was content to spend Halloween night ferociously napping under the vehicle.

Because of Cookie's lack of hearing, impaired vision, and arthritic agility, he had little interest in studying the cavalcade of trick-or-treaters who passed by. Most of the costumed kids remained on the sidewalk, which was a fair distance from Jim's car. As the evening began to wind down, an entourage of masked marauders caterwauled past our house. Even though their booty bags overflowed with treats, these chumps still lacked their fill of tricks.

Spying from my bedroom window, I monitored this mob, as they were about to execute their skullduggery. With soap in hand, the hot rod Chevy presented too much of a temptation for them. Just as these hooligans were within a few feet of the car, a chain began rattling. Next, a low pitched growl resonated in the darkness. Suddenly from beneath the car a bleary apparition appeared. The distant street lights reached only far enough to vaguely outline a wolfish silhouette. As this spirit hound's growl transcended to a more profound howl, bags of candy erupted into the chilly nighttime air. Fright turned to flight as the would-be tricksters ran for their lives. After the last of these ghouls disappeared into the twilight, Cookie celebrated his "spooktacular" serenade by feasting on the scattered spoils and once again tasting the rewards of being a contributing companion.

As the lesson learned here, be wary of old mansions. Confined within, there may exist many a haunting and hazard. Beware that outside its walls pitfalls and perils exist as well. Spare not your temperance of these elder dwellings, especially on that most hallowed of autumn evenings when spooks preside and tricks prevail. Most of all, stay clear of any daunting domain where instead of candy, you get a "Cookie."

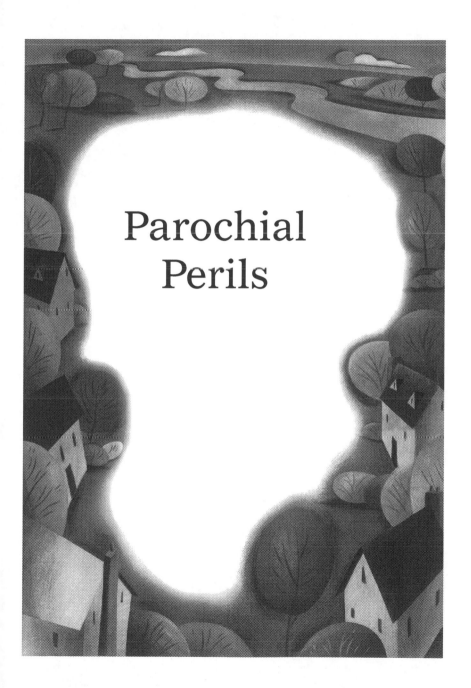

Parochial
Perils

Once upon a town untangled, confessions abounded as old habits were struck down. With the abandoning of sacred traditions, changes spewed forth with their own religious fervor. Resistance was futile. Those without faith did not have a prayer. Only time would tell whether this sacrificial shift ushered in revelation or revolution.

In my hometown, life was simple. We had only two religions: Catholic and other. Being part of the former, inoculated beliefs entitled me to the most glorious of heavenly graces. During my parochial upbringing, the good Sisters of Saint Joe's made it quite clear that being Catholic ensured divine priority. Those who did not embrace Catholicism surely were taking their chances. No doubt about it, I was truly blessed.

Although small, this hometown declared itself big enough to justify its own parochial hospital and elementary school. This non-secular theme transpired into separate winter sledding hills. It was well established that the steep grade leading down from the lofty heights of Saint Joseph's Church served a specific denomination. Not to be upstaged, the Lutheran church, perched on the west side, consecrated a holy hill of its own. It is not clear where the Methodist, Presbyterians, Congregationalists, Baptists, and others congregated for their sacred sledding. Nonetheless, religious strife constituted a slippery slope in the citizenry of our town.

The apocalyptic departure of the town's two Presbyterian churches still remains a mystery. At the height of an ongoing feud between the conventional Presbyterian and Welsh Presbyterian churches, the former suddenly and suspiciously burned to the ground. Coincidentally, the other church encountered the same fate a short time later. Apparently, these fire and brimstone ministries were taken to intense levels of heated exchange.

In the midst of this entrenched strife, members of different faiths were not given even a sporting chance to mingle. After an invitation from some friends, my dad joined in on a basketball game at the Congregational church. When one of the church elders discovered a Catholic boy shooting hoops on this denominational home court, he cried foul and booted my father from the game. When the Congregational pastor heard about this incident, he ordered the church elder to personally apologize to my father and his parents.

On the flip side, when my dad agreed to serve as best man at a non-Catholic wedding, the Catholic pastor stepped in and absolutely forbid him to do so. Due to an accident shortly before the wedding day, my dad was unable to attend the wedding and, therefore, avoided the possibility of excommunication. Caught up in this same holy war, my Norwegian grandfather scorned the non-Lutheran weddings of my mother and her brother. He strongly opposed non-Protestant blood transfusions when hospitalized. In his generation and the next, even the choice of dentists and doctors was based on religious preferences.

Although my school years began at the non-secular community kindergarten, it was a given that my following years would be spent at Saint Joseph's Catholic School. Along with satisfaction-guaranteed salvation, parochial school certainly had other advantages. For example, unlike the non-parochial "Publics," as we called them, Catholic school students received additional reflection time due to celebrations known as holy days. This usually meant attending Mass in the morning and sacrilegiously goofing off for the remainder of the day. The rest of our adolescence, however, was one of saintly hardships. The daily wear and tear of kneeling and genuflecting added to our suffering. Any notes sung out of tune during the afternoon hymn practices resulted in a well-pitched tongue lashing. Until the Saturday evening option for honoring the Sabbath became available, Sunday morning fishing, hunting, or football events represented unsanctified guilt trips when missing Mass. There was always resentment toward the Lutheran kids with their summer camp shenanigans. We felt grilled by the Protestants who feasted on Friday burgers all too often. Heck, many of them even got to watch *The Dirty Dozen* movie without pastoral permission.

Never did these easy-going evangelists ever endure the wrath of an ominous Mother Superior.

As an eight-year alumnus of Saint Joe's, my education resulted in the utmost enlightenment. Sister Merry Chorus taught me how to sing by firmly grabbing my hair and yanking upward for the high notes. This technique produced both harmony and heightened awareness. Like most nuns, Sister MC was kind hearted and well intentioned. Mind you, however, there were some immensely notable exceptions among both nun and lay teachers.

Under the crafty guise of an endearing grandmother, Ms. Alice served as our third-grade drill sergeant. The white hair and wire-rimmed spectacles of a Mrs. Claus fooled no one. Her most recognizable feature came by way of her enormous upper arms. The skin layers unfolded into what resembled bat wings. It was widely accepted that the incredible crack in her classroom blackboard had been caused by the guided impact of a former student's forehead. Whether this legend rang true or not, Ms. Alice symbolized a force to reckon with. Whacked knuckles, ear pulling, and supply-closet confinement were part and parcel to her domain. Those exposed to any of these corrective practices usually had it coming.

Adding to the intrigue of this widowed lay teacher was the fact her nearby home bordered what old timers called the Black Death Cemetery. Other references included the old burying ground. This inconspicuous graveyard rested just two blocks from Saint Joe's School. Dotted throughout the half-acre plot were mysterious depressions and mounds representing 136 victims of an Asiatic cholera epidemic that spread throughout this area in 1849 and again in 1851. On the fringe, several stone markers memorialized a tragic era when many locals abandoned their homes and moved to avoid exposure. Since then, the town simply grew around this eerie anomaly. Oftentimes, my friends and I utilized this forlorn lot as a shortcut to classes, unaware of the poor souls we were treading upon. Perhaps there was even the possibility that one of these internments directly related to a cracked blackboard. It seemed best to be prudent before antagonizing any teacher with a burial ground in her backyard.

Even more epic than Ms. Alice was the awe-inspiring Attila the Nun. Sister Attila may have been the world's tallest nun. Having an almost colorless complexion made one wonder as to whether this pious character had ever ventured into sunlight. Her high-rise headgear made her even more intimidating. Rarely did she smile or offer words of praise. Instead, Sister Attila often gestured by pointing long, spindly fingers as a sign of dissatisfaction. Someone spread a rumor that she belonged to an offshoot order of nuns known as the Merciless Sisters of Good God Almighty. At the conclusion of sixth grade, advancing students lived in dread. Her seventh grade classroom was perceived as sheer purgatory. I still recall the trauma of participating in the school's spelling bee under Sister Attila's charge. As a lowly sixth-grader, I nervously found myself thrust into competition with the seventh and eighth grade students. Lined up in front of Sister Attila, the scenario felt more like a firing squad drill as this nun took aim. After stumbling in the first round, I exited mortally wounded by her piercing glare and guttural command to leave immediately. Well tutored in the art of praying, my classmates and I sought divine intervention. Shortly before our seventh grade year was about to begin, we suddenly learned that Sister Attila had transferred to an unknown destination. Many substituted the word sanitarium. Truly we were blessed.

In the final year of elementary indoctrination, Sister Elder became my eighth-grade mentor. She desperately strived to instill moral character in every student and often repeated the phrase, "Dare to be different if different is right." Most of us only heard the part about being daring. Although Sister Elder attempted to portray a stern and serious personality, there was another side to this nun. Along with teaching eighth grade, she also served as the church organist. Sometimes while perched up in the choir loft, she became downright giddy once her fingers began dancing across the organ keyboard.

Sister Elder was much older than any of the previous nuns who had tutored us. As hard as she tried to make her age and experiences valuable to the learning process, it backfired at times. During a class on sex education, one of the students inquired, "Sister, what is sex really like?" Thus we learned, even nuns in their later years can blush beyond belief.

At a gymnasium practice, Sister Elder was attempting to choreograph the annual student graduation procession. My classmate Larry decided to test her patience by strutting and high stepping. Enraged by the sacrilegious nature of this behavior, Sister Elder amazed everyone by dashing hell-bent across the gym. Hobbled by severely arthritic knees, ankles, and hips, this aging nun was performing a miracle of mobility. Upon reaching Larry, she commenced beating on his back while shouting, "You brute, you brute, you brute. You're ruining everything!" Had her legs not been so debilitated, she may have kicked the devil out of him as well. Most likely, Larry would think twice before he dared to be different again.

Sometimes, radical irreverence is just a part of growing up Catholic. My father-in-law Al and his buddy habitually misbehaved in their years at parochial school. As a result, they would be locked into the supply closet for the remainder of the class period. Aware of this forthcoming outcome, the two trouble-makers prearranged to throw fielders' gloves and a baseball onto the school roof. Having spent previous confinements in the closet, they discovered a trap door leading to the roof. Using stacked boxes as steps, they ascended upward and honed their ball-playing skills while serving time.

The rooftop caper pales in comparison to what the father of my friend Mike did as a Catholic school student. His dad Jerome had a propensity for talking to others during the reading sessions. This was not tolerated by the disciplinarian nun teaching the class. After a torrid tantrum, she instructed Jerome to keep his eyes on the book. Showcasing downright obedience, he immediately responded by popping out his glass right eye and placing it upon the book. Unprepared and unaware of Jerome's unique situation, this rattled educator at first paused in silence and then retreated from the classroom to recompose her nerves.

Other students suffered more dire consequences for misbehaving. When one young man did not comply to an order to remove his jacket while in the classroom, he was escorted to the corridor, lifted onto the coat rack, and left hanging by the back of his jacket. Unable to free himself, he had to be rescued when class ended and recess began. Certain nuns were not to be confronted or contested.

Sometimes even a substitute teacher can become legendary. Take for example, Sister Armstrong, the stout and bespectacled nun with a lightening delivery. Sister Armstrong had an eccentric personality, which made her a mystery of sorts. You could never quite figure out her mood or gauge whether this

Sister was angry or pleased. As such, she was a master at catching students off guard. On one particular day, while filling in for the regular teacher, Sister Armstrong got tested by a student named Matt. Ignoring Sister Armstrong's repeated request to keep quiet and pay attention, Matt once more turned around to talk to the student seated behind him. Suddenly, Sister Armstrong grabbed a nearby blackboard eraser, cocked her arm, and released a perfect strike to the side of Matt's head. The resulting impact created a cloud of chalk dust that hovered all around Matt. As the dust finally settled, an imposing yellowish imprint could be seen along Matt's right temple. Everyone wanted to laugh at the outcome, however, no one dared for fear of becoming the next target. As insult to injury, Sister Armstrong then instructed Matt to retrieve the huge eraser and place it back onto the blackboard ledge. Chalk one up for divine intervention and the Franciscan nun with the precision pitching arm.

In terms of fear factors, none of the nuns compared with Father John, the parish pastor. This Irish priest could instill the "fear of God" in God as well. There seemed to be an eleventh commandment asserting, "Thou shall not dismay nor disobey this rector." During my early grade school years, Father John handed out the report cards. Seated at the teacher's desk and scanning the individual cards, he then summoned each student for a face-to-face consultation. Those who fared well garnered praise and blessings. As for the less gifted, they suffered a solemn wrath that often resulted in streaming tears and downtrodden demeanors. Never meant as meanness, this pastor's approach typified an era when divinity and discipline were tightly intertwined.

During my passage through adolescence, I viewed Father John as a typical crotchety and cantankerous old preacher. Nothing and no one could break down this spiritual leader. Years later, my dad shared with me that Father John had suffered from a long battle with cancer at this same time I came know this priest. It was then I realized the true grit and mettle of this man of the cloth.

Under the tutelage of Father John, becoming an altar boy meant entering Catholic boot camp. Precision drills were practiced while learning rituals and memorizing exacting refrains. Cadence, posturing, and expressions demanded perfection. What made it even more difficult was learning everything in Latin. Like many of our peers, Mike and I became so devout in our altar boy pursuits that we collected holy cards like cherished baseball cards. I still remember trading Saint Jude and Immaculate Mary for a coveted Saint Francis of Assisi.

Just as Mike and I completed training, an avalanche of changes rumbled through the Catholic landscape. All Latin recitations changed to English. In the boldest of moves, women were no longer required to wear head coverings when attending Mass. The upper altitude habits worn by the good Sisters were downsized and revealed that the sisters actually had hair and ears. In what came to be a risqué rebellion, many nuns now exchanged their heavyweight robes for white blouses and ankle-exposing skirts. Apparently this had an unexpected impact, because our new seventh grade teacher vacated the convent the following year and married a church trustee. Of course, this minor scandal paled in comparison to the major shock created when the popular assistant pastor came out of the closet.

Abrogating the no meat on Fridays doctrine created new alternatives to the all-you-can-eat seafood feasts of gluttony. Other sacred traditions were touched by this liberal conspiracy as well. Altars were repositioned so that the priests now faced the congregation throughout Mass. By way of an orthopedic revelation, standing replaced kneeling during Holy Communion services. No longer did the sacrament of confession allow us to observe who was confessing and how much. Instead of lining up in the aisles and filing one-by-one into the confessionals, the church adopted a group pardoning known as Open Confession. Forthcoming on the horizon were reforms such as discontinuing the strange practice of dropping money into a slotted box and lighting candles in order to expedite a relative or friend from purgatory. Even Sister Elder's musical mastery began being upstaged at times by guest cantors and guitarists.

In the midst of these diverging times, the day finally arrived when Mike and I were officially installed as altar boys. Our first assignment involved the sunrise service at the hospital chapel. We did not know the hospital housed a chapel, let alone that daily Mass was conducted so early every morning. Ours, however, was not to question but to serve, and so we did. Mike lived half a block from me and two blocks north of the hospital. Our sojourn to the hospital followed the same path taken decades ago by my paternal grandmother. During an early December blizzard, she suddenly went into labor and had no choice but to trudge by foot through the snowstorm. Within one block of the hospital, she could venture no further. When the hospital was notified, a stout local nun renowned for feats of strength came to her rescue. Sister Hercules carried my grandmother to the hospital. As a result, my father Robert was brought into this world. Once again, Catholicism affirmed itself as a strong-armed religion.

Adjacent to the Catholic cemetery, Saint Joseph's Hospital was similar to an ecclesiastical Wal-Mart that served every need from birth to burial. At one time, this complex operated a farm on its grounds. Franciscan nuns raised produce and poultry to nourish the patients. Just south of this infirmary, there was an immense stockyard of cattle and cow pies. Its presence was well known whenever southeastern winds began to bluster. The result led to an odious aroma with medical implications. For those who happened to be hospitalized and aroused by the sensual nature of these nearby stockyards, it simply meant they were alive and well on the road to recovery.

It was a calm and windless day when Mike and I arrived at dawn for our inaugural hospital assignment. As such, the only aroma to stir our senses was that of disinfectant. Being of vintage character, the hospital's high ceilings and long, dimly lit corridors created an eerie aura. Wandering about, we eventually found our way to the chapel. Upon entering this small room with an altar and six rows of oaken pews, a patriarchal chaplain greeted us. Mike and I were guided into the sanctuary to don our cassocks and frocks. After discussing where to position ourselves during the Mass, I settled on taking the left side of the altar. Mike agreed to the right, which meant he would have a more active role during Holy Communion.

As the chapel service began, I was awed at the assembled congregation. Everyone appeared older than the quaint chaplain himself. I was looking at a reunion of religious relics. In a morbid revelation, it now occurred to me why the cemetery resided nearby. This sight became even more profound as the attendees lined up for communion. Even though these extreme elders were only steps away from the chaplain, it took an eternity for each one to shuffle forward. I silently said a prayer of thanks that Mike had agreed to hold the communion paten, a wood-handled brass plate placed under the chin of each recipient. Under no circumstances would the round wafer host be allowed to fall and touch the ground. Dictated by Catholic doctrine, the host could only touch the hands of an ordained priest and the tongue of the recipient. As such, standing on each side of the chaplain, Mike and I now served as astute observers to the tongues, throats, and dental work of aging anatomies.

Out of the corner of my eye, I caught a glimpse of the last member in line. This old man appeared to be the ancient of elders. Remnants of gray hair straddled above a face furrowed with deep time lines. Bearing wrinkles so defined and numerous, his skin resembled a Ruffles potato chip. His complexion was colorless and his eyes seemed hollow. Only a miniscule amount of flesh still clung to the duffer's bones. His tweed jacket may have fit snugly decades ago, yet now appeared to have swallowed him whole with his feeble body dangling inside. This codger's entire well being balanced precariously on the wooden cane that supported him. Like a war prisoner on a death march, each step forward seemed to be his last. Part of me wanted to look away, yet at the same time, I felt compelled to cheer this geezer on. Slowly, with determination, he made it. Now positioned in front of the chaplain, he lifted his chin up and cocked his head backward. Then, with lifeless eyes peering upward and his mouth wide open for reception of the holy host, it happened. Without warning, the upper denture descended from his mouth and landed dead center onto the paten held by Mike. Although this man was falling apart right before our eyes, Mike and I immediately froze and dared not to make eye contact with each other. While we did our best to look away, the chaplain never flinched as the denture was refitted in place. No amount of tenacious training from Father John had prepared us for this ordeal. Like the old patron, we were in serious jeopardy of losing our grip on this first assignment.

During the remainder of the Mass, it felt as though we had held our breaths for eternity. At the point of almost hyperventilating, we finally exited the hospital. While heading home, the suppressed laughter became uncontrollable. Tears streamed down our faces as we reached Mike's house. Just before departing, Mike looked at me and said, "You know what's even funnier? Tomorrow you get to hold the paten."

With sobering thoughts of declining dentures and images of the living dead etched in my mind, I plodded home. Throughout the rest of the day, this pious journey of mine bewildered me. There would be trials and tribulations, this I knew. It just never entered into my wildest imagination that being raised Catholic would lead to such fallout. Thank God for the strength of character instilled in me by Father John, Sister Elder, Ms. Alice, and all the others at St. Joe's, who shepherd our souls.

Ruffled
Feathers

Once upon a town untangled, an untimely death was precipitated by the dereliction of two misguided souls. Unaware of the repercussions, these hapless thrill seekers had been exploited by the pursuit of fame and fortune. In the end, their ambitions transpired into a horrifying aftermath that they hoped would remain buried forever.

It is not difficult to hoodwink or bamboozle young minds. All it takes is a little boredom and a fair share of yearning on the part of victims to foster obvious exploitation. As such, the cunning deliberations of advertised promises and creative scripts lure the innocent and idealistic to unscrupulous adventure. Perhaps that is why my eighth grade classmate Bob and I did what we did.

What is about to be confessed is not solely my and/or Bob's fault. Some of the blame belongs to my paternal grandparents. Grammy Agnes encouraged me to read far too many books and magazines. Enticed by her impressive library room, she influenced me even further with Greyhound bus trips to big city bookstores. As for Grampy John's involvement, I fell under the spell of tinkering and transformation at his nearby Cities Service gas station. This lethal combination thus cultivated both a far-fetched imagination and way too many capers.

Not only did my grandparents reside just across the street from my home, they provided access to one of the first color TV's in town and an endless supply of Fritos. Even better, their ranch house encompassed an expansive basement that became the perfect staging area for teenage tomfoolery. However, tomfoolery gone awry soon translates into skullduggery, which is exactly what happened on a Saturday morning in April.

Had my frail grandparents descended the stairway and entered their basement on this doomsday, it may have adversely altered their golden years. By doing so, they would have encountered something far too ghastly, too hideous, and too unexpected for the emotional and physical condition of their fragile senior status. A gruesome experiment of blood, carnage, and downright juvenile delinquency was in full progress in the very midst of their home.

Marooned within this dimly lit bunker was an old dilapidated pool table. The warped contours and shoddy felt surface rendered it almost useless as a game table. Instead, it was now covered with newspapers and transformed for a much different cause. Centered on this table was a motionless body oozing blood upon the underlying newspapers. Two shadowy figures hovered over this corpse. As much as I hate to admit it, my friend Bob and I were the duo who stood witness to this sacrilege. The peril in progress simply began as an innocent endeavor to ward off monotony yet ended with the consequential memory that haunts me to this very day.

At this point in our young lives, Bob and I were impressionable and easily influenced. The two of us eagerly trusted most of what we read or heard. None of this would have happened had we just disregarded the magazine ad. In our small hometown, however, it was far too difficult to ignore the promises of unlimited riches.

Sometimes I look back on what conspired here and label it a religious rebellion. As devout Catholic altar boys, Bob and I needed to experience more than the rigid doldrums of our parochial upbringing. There was an incurable adolescent need to encounter the dark side. Why else would a wholesome character like Bob engage in the Igor-like behavior of bringing a cadaver to this underground asylum? I never interrogated Bob regarding how this lifeless form met its demise, nor did I want to know. Bob did his part and now it was time to do mine.

Following intense study and explicit instructions, I sawed through multiple rib bones, spliced open the chest cavity, and began extracting all that was embodied. Not taking as long as anticipated, I soon found myself in the second phase of cleaning out the blood and all remaining materials from this hollowed-out corpse. Equipped with a brain spoon and bone scraper, Bob took over and completed work on the head, which included plucking the eyes out. Per instructions, we coated the entire figure inside and out with a formula of Borax and powdered Calorax. Before long, we progressed to the final stage of reconfiguring the body by stuffing the interior with excelsior, aligning wires, and stitching all previous incisions. Although this ordeal consumed several hours, we completed the necessary work without any breaks. Time was of the essence and everything needed to be finished before any unexpected visitors ventured into this makeshift morgue.

The time finally came for us to step back and marvel at our creation. There was an extensive pause, during which we desperately refrained from reactions. While containing our gasps and groans, we now recoiled at a fowl so incredibly diabolical that it no longer resembled anything of this world. The concocted creature peering back at us had once been a common pigeon. This

squandered squab had forever lost the identity of a recognizable species. If taken outside and left as road kill, this despicable creation would have repulsed even the most desperate of starving scavengers. Blackened by its chemical bath, the bird appeared to have been pulled from an oil slick. This freak was far from the masterpiece illustrated in our easy step-by-step *Taxidermy for Fun and Profit* manual.

According to the *Boy's Life* magazine ad that enticed such a perverted project, this was supposed to lead to a career of recognition and riches. Instead, Bob and I now possessed a boogie bird whose neck was double its normal length. The beak protruded in a fiendish fashion as did both bugged-out glass eyes. Its body had been stuffed and stretched to butterball proportions. Ruffled feathers stuck out in haphazard patterns as if this critter had unsuccessfully challenged a live electrical wire. Making a candid observation, one might guess that this feathered fatality expired from an overdose of steroid-laden birdseed.

Without question, Bob and I now had to contend with disposing of the Frankenbird. To end this innocent, yet sinister, ordeal, it was agreed that this alien life-form must be immediately buried and concealed for eternity. After placing the pitiful pigeon back into the gunnysack from which it came, we then cleaned up all remaining evidence and quickly departed. Without needing my assistance, Bob sauntered off to entomb our efforts of this grim affair.

To this day, I have never asked Bob where he buried the embalmed entity. Perhaps centuries from now, an amateur archeologist or paleontologist will unearth this creation and be heralded for the remarkable discovery of an unknown ancient species. As a result, the fame and fortune that eluded two adventurous lads, would ceremoniously surface in a National Geographic special or PBS series. Foregoing any liable legacy, I can only hope that the scientific methods of the era do not allow this discovery to be traced back to Bob and me. Until then, there's no dire need to uncover or recover the wretched truth.

An overrated adage states that if at first you do not succeed, try, try again. As such, I showed Bob another advertisement. It claimed that by raising Silver Mist Chinchillas for pleasure and profit, you could earn thousands. However, for whatever reason, Bob no longer seemed interested in becoming rich and famous. Too bad, there was still plenty of room for prosperity in Grampy's basement.

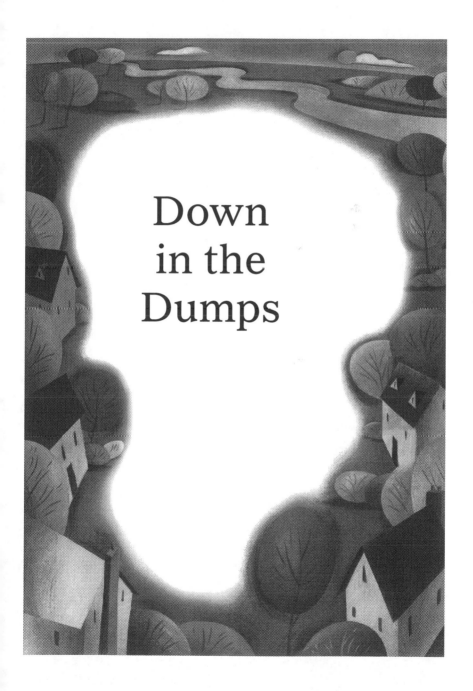

Down in the Dumps

Once upon a town untangled, in the aftermath of gunfire, glass shattered and rats scattered. Without realizing the dire consequences of their actions, a young duo of trigger-happy hooligans destroyed a treasure deeply cherished by their elders. This sad and sorrowful outcome should perhaps be forgotten yet will now be rekindled for its stone-cold sober verocity.

Although this story hinges on death and destruction, it also focuses on the lively legacies of two well-known duffers who wandered the streets in differing directions. Both were hardcore laborers and loners of sorts. One was driven in a peculiar way, while the other marched about with an axe to grind.

Small towns are just big enough when there is a town hall, town dump, and town drunk. One represents a beginning, the other an ending, and the third a reality. My hometown was certainly bolstered by all three. An uninspiring town hall was located on the main street. On the eastern outskirts lay the smoldering town dump. Equally dispersed throughout this community was the town's contingent of heavy drinkers. It would be extremely unfair to christen but one as the true town drunk. This unheralded title was in contention by many. While there was a cadre of well-established contenders, formidable newcomers were always emerging.

In regard to town halls, there's little to share about the one in my hometown. When the neighboring Crystal Theater went up in flames during the historic business district fire, this town hall survived as downtown's most mundane fixture. Lacking Gothic pillars and ornate arches, the town hall was a humble brick building, fronted by gray concrete steps and iron railings. The quaint cupola that once graced its rooftop had sadly disappeared. Akin to the town itself, not much ever happened here. Except for the occasional villager wandering in and out of the town hall, it was notably void of both character and characters. However, this was not the case for the nearby taverns frequented by the likes of the Chihuahua Lady and John Deere Jimmy. As resident pub patrons, these two were contrasting characters. While one exhibited showmanship, the other was more timid and less visible when it came to hooch-nipping habits.

The Chihuahua Lady was a neighbor who lived two houses up the block and across the street. Her house was a neatly kept bungalow on a corner lot. During the late morning hours each week, she embarked on a routine of strolling downtown with her leashed pint-sized pooch leading the way. What appeared to be nothing more than a commonplace promenade with the family pet suddenly changed in scope as she headed home. The real reason for the customary walkabouts lay hidden within the long narrow brown paper bag that she clutched slyly in her left hand. One had only to observe the empty bottles nestled within her street-side trash can as confirmation of the bag's contents.

In a town this small, there was simply no room for secrets. What you did not see firsthand, you were sure to encounter through the grapevine of gossip. Such was the curse placed on the Chihuahua Lady. Neighborhood conversations babbled about a lonely woman who often sought companionship from the bottle during her husband's long road trips as a traveling salesman. It was even rumored that her Chihuahua imbibed as well.

Rarely was the Chihuahua Lady seen outside her home, except for her habitual jaunts for the jolly juice. Whenever doing so, she would dress to the tee in what appeared to be her Sunday best. Crowned upon her head rested an elegant hat covering the once dark hair now gilded white gold. At times, she even wore beaded formal gloves to match her dress shoes. Bright red lipstick often contrasted with her aged and pale complexion. On the coldest days, a full-length fur coat served as part of her winter ensemble. As part of a generation in which housewives were often marooned without a car or driver's license, sometimes just a mere walk can become a special event to uncork when you are bottled in and need to bottle down.

John Deere Jimmy was the opposite of the Chihuahua Lady. Even though I never formally met JDJ, I knew him well. Jimmy was a community icon, easily distinguished by his mode of transportation. His life's story reads like that of the tortoise and the hare. As a younger man, Jimmy was a rabbit dashing about whenever the spontaneous urge for liquid grain afflicted him. These pursuits eventually resulted in far too many mobile mishaps. When his driver's license was finally revoked, Jimmy literally switched gears to become a turtle. Being a conscientious and innovative imbiber, Jimmy lawfully refrained from putting himself behind the wheel of any licensed-required vehicle. Instead, he became a patient patron at the helm of a lawn tractor. Slowly but surely, he routinely motored along the roadway shoulders to the nearest watering hole. As a tractor tortoise, Jimmy reached his coveted destinations with slow-paced persistence.

Although area farmers revered Jimmy as a hard-working hired hand when sober, his dominant vocation was that of a professional consumer. Jimmy's drinking habits generated a generous amount of local notoriety. Just as the Chihuahua Lady's jaunts, Jimmy's ventures ripened well on the grapevine. If there was a need to know more about Jimmy, you simply relied on a communications network. Its effectiveness and expansiveness rivaled today's Internet. In this era, it was called the party line. By simply picking up a residential phone, there was an instant connection to the local information highway. No dial up or e-mail address was needed. By listening in long enough, one was sure to hear about the latest Jimmy sighting. As a form of communal espionage, the party line locked onto Jimmy like satellite surveillance and fed directly to the ungracious gadabouts. When it came to talk on these telephone lines, the righteous teetotalers were especially hard on Jimmy.

Wheeling about on the downsized John Deere and clad in his trademark bib overalls, Jimmy became a perennial of the local landscape. Viewed more as a novelty rather than a nuisance, it was somewhat taboo to poke fun at him. As a sobering lesson to youthful gawkers, Jimmy evolved into a rolling billboard on alcohol education. While most kids relished running alongside Jimmy on his tractor, no one grew up wanting to follow in his path. Swerving and singing along his habitual routes, a message reverberated far louder than Jimmy's garbled voice or whining engine.

While most lubricated lushes prefer to make it nobody's business as to how much or how often they consume, the town had one particular sour mash celebrity who made boozing a notable part of his enterprise. Footloose Frank served many years as the community's foremost shoe peddler. He did so during an era when this municipality was the only one in the county to maintain prohibition until the early 1960s.

With little competition to his shoe store, Frank had little to worry about customers or image. However, as in any retail endeavor, there were those monotonous lulls when sales slowed. Frank then relied on other passions to fill the void. As such, Frank contrived an ongoing arrangement with an out-of-town tavern to which he delivered a number of empty shoe boxes. When necessary, a single shoe box would be returned to his store. Inside the box was a precious bottle of Kentucky's finest distilled spirits.

For Frank, whiskey and his trombone went hand in hand. The more he drank, the more he played the boisterous instrument. The jargon for this style of musical freelancing was known as "frisking the whiskers or licking the chops." His jazzed-up stupor was Frank's version of a shoe horn serenade. What was music to Frank's ears, clearly blasted a warning sign to anyone seeking new shoes. If someone was truly in need of being fitted for shoes, it was probably best to stay clear when the sounds of Frank's tumultuous trombone filled the air.

Even though Jimmy and Frank were what you might call "happy go lucky" drinkers, a lesson learned at age ten taught me to stay clear of any boozers. One day I decided to sit on the steps outside the auto parts store where my dad worked and wait for him to return from a sales call. Next door was a popular bar called the Red Room. While peering down the street, I watched an obviously inebriated patron stagger out from this tavern. Barrel-chested and well into senior status, this big man struggled to keep his balance. As he approached me, my gaze cast downward in order to avoid any eye contact. Suddenly, a pair of worn out work boots halted in front of me. Before even having the chance to look up, a pair of muscular hands clamped onto my shoulders. I then found myself being lifted off the ground. In a state of shock, I momentarily froze and did not know what to do. Looking up, I encountered the stench of alcohol and a gravelly voice that blurted, "I am going to hug you. I am going to kiss you. I am going to kill you." Thus said the man and then dropped me and ambled away laughing.

Retreating into the store, I quickly told my dad's co-worker about what had just happened. Almost simultaneously, my dad and the police showed up just minutes later. Both seemed to know quite well the drunkard I described. As for the fate of this bozo, I never did find out what became of him. For a very long time, I shied well away from this area and never saw the old codger again.

Prevalent in far too many places, boozing created a common lifestyle in our town. For some, it became a patriotic practice. Despite the municipal prohibition on hard liquor, beer joints served as an oasis, especially for those who had returned from WWII and the Korean conflict. Local veterans on the GI Bill formed what they called the 52/20 Club. Each Friday after returning from the county courthouse with a weekly twenty dollar pension check, they gathered together to stimulate the economy of nearby watering holes. It was a military convoy swaggering in and staggering out.

Any need for hard liquor required a more cautious approach. Nonetheless, an established bootlegger operated a full-fledged still just one block from my grandfather's home. One of the moonshiner's main customers was the local pharmacy, which kept a ready supply of distilled goods under the counter for medicinal purposes. The downtown hotel, which also served as a stage and bus stop, was also a loyal customer of the bootlegger. Patrons of the hotel, selective travelers, and favored cronies were able to partake in its backroom speakeasy, despite the claim of being a temperance establishment.

Almost every community has at least one overindulging elder, who serves as a public nuisance. Hereabouts, that role belonged to Snooky. Whether intoxicated or just plain crazy, this curmudgeon wobbled around town while grumbling profusely at bystanders, introducing obscenities to the younger generation, and thrusting his cane wildly at anyone in close proximity. Although scary at times, old Snooky was easily outmaneuvered and more of a make-believe menace than a genuine threat.

Should Snooky have gone off the deep end, there existed a special destination for him. Although referred to by some as the county funny farm and by others as the old folks' home, the secluded enclave just west of town, carried a very distinct title in days past. Starkly posted on its gated archway were the words "INSANE ASYLUM". Guards, iron fences, and barred windows added to its foreboding nature. Seeming more like inmates than patients, those escorted here either as mentally inept or needing serous detox, often experienced treatments such as being wrapped in icy wet blankets, receiving knuckle sandwiches, or confinement in the rubber room. Still in existence today, both the means and mission of this locale have fortunately changed over the years.

Not to be excluded, local juveniles had their own drinking exploits as well. The older brother of my classmate, Mike, boasted one of the most novel approaches to boozing. Somehow, he gained possession of a casket that converted to a makeshift cooler by filling it with ice and bottled beer. Mounted on a small trailer, the casket was then escorted around town to wherever needed. At times, this ghoulish ice box, ended up at a place known as "The Quarry". Located northeast of town and at the end of a dirt road, this secluded gravel pit became a well-established hideout for partying youth and drunks-in-training.

Town halls and town drunks are simply not enough; these are easy to come by. In order to be truly complete, there must be a genuine town dump. Due to good fortune, my hometown had one of the best. Town halls and town drunks don't vary much from one small community to another. What they generally have in common is a weathered facade, limited finances, and a desperate need for serious rehabilitation. Town dumps, however, are quite special and the one belonging to my hometown was no exception. It had far more character than the town hall and town drunks combined.

Many folks around here do not realize that the site of the original town dump was located where the high school now resides. It was bulldozed and steamrolled for the sake of education. As such, my sophomore, junior, and senior years were totally based on garbage. However, the most memorable dump festered just southeast of the public cemetery. The scent of this refuge of refuse alerted a person to its proximity without setting eyes on it. Being downwind from the town dump was an aromatic adventure and olfactory assault. It was made possible by the fact that this depository represented a genuine dump rather than a politically correct landfill. It embodied a rubbish domain of nobility and dimension. Instead of being plowed under and hidden beneath the earth, this dump put garbage in its place—one rotting pile on top of another. As a result, the artistry and aroma of its treasures were left exposed for everyone to experience. So valuable was this treasure, the dump had its very own guardian known as Junkyard George.

Like John Deere Jimmy, old George was a community icon, yet much more mysterious and compelling. This was created in part by his venturing about with an axe in hand. George lived near the east edge of town, just one block from a tangle of woods called Black's Grove. In many ways, Black's Grove was reminiscent of the *Wizard of Oz* scene in which Dorothy encountered the Cowardly Lion. It was dark, eerie, and shrouded by a dense canopy of treetops. When I crept through it, the urge to repeat "Lions and tigers and bears, oh my" was quite strong. The deeper one ventured into Black's Grove, the darker it became. It was a spooky enclave, made even more so because it was the hallowed haunt of Junkyard George and located adjacent to the dump.

This diligent scrounger ventured routinely throughout Black's Grove en route to the trash troves. At the town dump, George would poke his axe about while scavenging through newly deposited prospects. Upon discovery, any salvageable treasures were escorted by way of a gunny sack or wheelbarrow to his small brick home. The items were then added to the intriguing treasury that barricaded his yard. Although his surroundings took on the look of a never-ending rummage sale, no one dared to criticize or contest George's collection of rescued relics. Holding his ground as the rest of the community grew up around him, he was our designated down-home hillbilly.

Fortified within his salvage-yard shelter, there was general consensus not to provoke the inhabitant and architect who literally walked about with a real axe to grind. In many ways, George was a man ahead of his time, a preservationist and pioneer of recycling. By today's standards, his booty of odds and ends would now be coveted as valuable antiques and recoverable riches.

A widower, Junkyard George was certainly a man of mystery and reclusive enough that few who lived outside the southeast side of this small town were aware of the old hermit. His usual attire consisted of suspendered dungarees and a plaid flannel shirt with the sleeves rolled up to reveal the gray woolies underneath. On colder days, a red mackinaw coated George's spindly frame. The wide brim of his floppy Jed Clampett hat concealed just about every facial feature except for the salt and pepper whiskers that mapped George's narrow chin. It was not a well-manicured beard but rather a month or two worth of scruff.

Without a vehicle, George relied on his work boots to travel about. From time to time, he worked at my grandfather's Cities Service Gas Station. George took on the laboring chore of cleaning out the grease pits. It was a solitary task that suited him during the late night hours. However, his primary vocation seemed to be one of living off the land.

Avoiding any social limelight, George was rarely seen other than during his treks to the town dump. Sometimes, he would emerge from Black's Grove carrying his rifle and a fistful of squirrels. On occasion, one might catch a backyard glimpse of George honing his axe on a huge rotating whetstone. Attached to a treadle, the stone wheel spun rapidly as George pressed down on its pedal and angled the axe head across its surface. As such, the axe wielded by George never suffered a dull moment. Aside from this activity and some ambitious wood splitting, George spent little time outside his hermitage or away from his storied collection of cast offs. Although this place desperately yearned for a Martha Stewart makeover, it commanded the reverence of a sacred burial ground where all must remain undisturbed.

Like most of the local kids, I was fascinated by old George and one day decided to trace his path through Black's Grove. Persuaded by my friend Kirk, we conjured up the plot of making a target-shooting trip to the town dump. Hearing tales about the dump's enormous rats, we pledged to vanquish the vermin. This was to be

a gallant crusade and nothing less. With rifles in hand, Kirk and I marched through the neighborhoods and headed for Black's Grove. Along the way, we passed by George's home. Guided by our keen senses and a distant fragrance, finding this enchanted forest and the dump beyond was a simple task. Traversing quickly, we were more concerned about an old George encounter than anything else lurking within this shadowy forest.

It did not take long for our noses to zero in on the destination we were pursuing. In short order, Kirk and I found ourselves amid the smoking residue of garbage and rat lairs. The only things missing from these smoldering ruins were the rats. Either they had escaped prior to our arrival or were sinisterly hiding in ambush. Before we could ponder this dilemma, Kirk shouted out that treasure had been discovered. It was an understatement. To my amazement, Kirk had uncovered two cases of Pabst Blue

Ribbon and several bottles of Jack Daniels. Even though there were a few broken bottles in each case, this did not seem like reason enough to abandon such valuable bounty. It was now up to the two of us to make proper use of this staggering find.

It is easy to understand how Kirk eventually became an attorney in years to come. He was always methodical and decisive in his actions. As such, I relied on him to bring justice to this delicate matter. Without hesitation, Kirk carefully removed each beer bottle while examining the contents and shaking it vigorously. He then set each bottle down in a precise line formation. After a complete inspection of the second case and repeating his maneuvers, Kirk now instructed me to step back a number of paces and inspect this makeshift lineup. As the two of us contemplated our next move, Kirk echoed his final command to commence firing. What happened next was a volatile fireworks of foam. Each time one of us nailed a bottle, its pressurized contents exploded in response to this firing squad execution. Blown to smithereens, frothy beer and brown glass lay scattered everywhere. Next in line were the bottles of Jack Daniels. Intoxicated by the outcome of such an assault, we experienced our first underage blast with booze.

Kirk and I never had the opportunity to skirmish with the notorious rats on that day at the dump. Nonetheless, bursting the brew-filled bottles did not leave us disappointed. It is hard to say what Junkyard George would have thought of this shattering escapade. On the other hand, had John Deere Jimmy or Footloose Frank known what conspired on this eventful afternoon, we might have been cursed for eternity. However, thanks to a vow of secrecy by two young sharpshooters, word of this down in the dumps ordeal eluded both the opinionated party line and wrath of the local liquidators.

This venerable dump has now been leveled and currently serves as the foundation for a new subdivision. I often wonder what surprises are unearthed as these homeowners plant trees and dig their backyard gardens. Perhaps someone's discovery will include a well-preserved pigeon among the shards of glass.

Really
Cool
Studs

Once upon a town untangled, temperatures were rising. Summer had finally arrived, and romance filled the air. The time had come for young males to do what young males must do. Chauvinism and chivalry were about to take center stage. Manhood was looming and there would be no turning back. The rite of passage that would transform rambunctious lads transformed and recast themselves as endearing macho dudes could not be denied.

With eight years of parochial school behind us, my friends and I stood on the brink of greatness. Summer dawned and with its waning sun-filled days would come a new dimension called public school. This time of passage demanded that we prepare ourselves and finally learn all that the good sisters of Saint Joe's had cleverly withheld from our ecumenical elementary educations. It was time as well to stretch the bestowed boundaries of holiness and hallelujahs by leaning a little bit more toward unencumbered devilish passions. In this era of reckoning, it was now or never to escape our cloistered lives and become really cool studs.

Combining the flexed muscles of our virile brainpower, a plan was put into motion. The summer season must begin with a camping trip to our favorite swimming hole at the nearby state park. Lacking a tent, we turned to ingenuity. A friend's dad parked his huge feed delivery truck at the campsite and left it there for the weekend. This would readily serve as home base for Studville. Up to eight campers could toss sleeping bags into its rear box and doze under the shelter of a canvas canopy. For each of us, it was our very first bachelor pad. Independent of any adult supervision, this represented paradise. All that we needed now were members of the opposite sex to captivate and charm with our imposing personalities. To succeed as local yokels, our hopes and dreams required out-of-town gals who were easily impressionable and considerably naive.

Although I alleged we were free of adult supervision, the word parental should have been used instead. Not only did a medley of park rangers patrol the campgrounds, one in particular represented the most formidable of foes. The middle school principal, who would serve as our commandant in the fall, worked part time as a ranger each summer. It did not take long for this enforcer nicknamed "Cookie Man" to introduce himself at our campsite and issue a few precautionary warnings. With no tolerance for teenage tendencies, he was already perturbed about the firecrackers being innocently tossed into our campfire. Starting off with a bang, this paled in comparison to what would later develop into a major meltdown.

Named after the first territorial governor, the state park was comprised of more than five thousand acres of reclaimed farmsteads with two separate campgrounds and two man-made lakes. Lacking transportation and thus mobility, we took up residence at what locals cleverly called the old lake. Its campground was in closer proximity to a beach than the new lake campground. All of us were more than familiar with the new lake's deadly environment of mishaps and man-eaters. The new lake was more of a fishing destination than a swimming hole. As the larger and deeper of the two lakes, vultures often hovered overhead as monsters dwelled within its depths. Saber-toothed leviathans infested this lake and threatened all who entered it. Some referred to these fiendish fish as muskies. The legend still lives on of one unsuspecting victim, whose foolishness resulted in a brutal blood bath.

On a midsummer day, an off-duty police officer from a nearby town embarked on an angling outing with his girlfriend. After launching their boat into the new lake, they had little success catching anything during the morning hours. As boredom and rising temperatures set in, the police officer decided to cool off by dangling his bare right foot in the water. Annoyed by this maneuver, a nearby muskie surfaced and latched onto his big toe. In a knee-jerk response, he flailed his leg upward and into the boat. This did nothing to disengage the scaly predator. It flopped about in the bottom of the boat while continuing to mangle the police officer's toe. After considerable effort, he managed to extricate the fish from its death grip. With blood spewing about, it was time to call it a day and seek medical attention. Being such an outrageous ordeal, the police officer kept the muskie as evidence. In checking out the story, the area game warden was anything but sympathetic. Not only did he charge the fisherman with an illegal fishing method, he cited the poor chap for possession of a muskie under the legal length, which was a whopping forty inches. Justice may be swift, but it also can be reversed. In response to public pressure, the charges were dropped against this angler who had already suffered enough. Among other things, this gripping episode proved that toe dipping, as well as skinny dipping, were not advisable activities in these waters.

Something even more sinister lay along the shores near the far end of the new lake. Numerous times while fishing this area with my youngest brother Scott, we became horridly subjected to vicious attacks that left us scratching for answers. An invisible menace maimed our legs with festering purple welts. We later learned that this skullduggery was the work of chiggers, blood sucking mites that lay eggs in a person's skin and wreak havoc for weeks. It's as gross as it sounds. After too many assaults by these malicious midgets, we abandoned this area for several seasons and moved on to another lake outside the park. Although this retreat led to a successful escape from the nasty chiggers, a new and different threat awaited us.

Accompanied on the next outing by our brother Tom, he immediately hooked a largemouth bass and began reeling it in. Unexpectedly, a demented water snake simultaneously shot out from the rocky bank on which we were standing. It then skimmed across the lake surface, latched on to the tail of the hooked fish, and commenced a tug of war on top of the water. Thank goodness it was not one of the deadly Timber rattlers that still slither about this area, despite the attempts of bounty hunters. Nonetheless, no freakish fiascos like these ever occurred at the park's old lake, which always lent itself more to tranquility than trauma.

The reasons for choosing the old lake for our weekend retreat are obvious. Before scouting the campground and heading to the beach, someone suggested that we bolster our bravado by engaging in liquid persuasion. According to one of the more influential members of our gang, you could actually get drunk by poking holes into a watermelon and sucking out its contents through a straw. To our formative intellects, this sounded like a no-brainer dash into a brave new world. Having both watermelons and straws at our bidding, the imbibing began without hesitation. It was not easy drawing the juicy melon through small straws, yet we persisted and soon found ourselves growing a wee-bit giddy. That was for the sum of our intoxicating adventure that never quite reached the anticipated level of inebriation. Years later, we learned that a quart of vodka must first be spiked into the melon for this endeavor to accomplish any staggering results.

With this debacle behind us, we decided to journey down to the beach and stake our mandated claims. It took no time at all to spot three unfamiliar young ladies sunning themselves. With all the swagger of eighth grade graduates, stud time had arrived. Strutting forward, we circled the girls and introduced ourselves as the official beach patrol. We then learned that these sirens were somewhat older and from out of state. In stud terms, this was the mother lode. Foreigners to our homeland, these gals would be both easily impressed and enamored. Between now and the weekend's conclusion, we faced the prospect of unlimited possibilities.

Playing it cool, we patiently sat on the beach while sharing with these gals all the incredible achievements of our adolescent lives. These were big city girls, alone in the wilderness. To comfort and quell their fears, my friends and I pledged to serve as their noble guardians in this savage land. Sensing their awe of our honorable intentions, we invited them to stop by our campsite later in the evening. After exchanging information on each other's campsite numbers, the temptress trio departed to get ready for an evening of exhilaration. Because it was still early in the day, the stud contingent decided to swim awhile before returning to our campsite. Hyped up at this juncture with anticipation and expectations, we really needed to burn off a whole lot of energized enthusiasm.

Approximately two hours later, as the sunburns set in on our pale unseasoned bodies, we noticed the clouds of an approaching storm. Heeding the warnings of rumbling thunder, we retreated to the bath house and changed into our camping duds. It was a fair trek from the beach to the campground, so we began jogging to beat out the impending storm. To our misfortune, the storm outran us. Dashing to the campground, all of us were drenched by the time we jumped into the back of the truck. In addition to a thorough soaking, this storm also brought a rapid drop in the temperature. Cold and shaking from our submersions, there was no way to warm ourselves around a blazing campfire in the continuing downpour. Our only option now was to strip down and warm up in our sleeping bags. In a frenzy to do so, we were completely unaware of the anguish that would soon besiege us.

The first two guys to bolt into their bags began emitting blood curdling screams. A third did likewise as he crawled into his bag. In a rabid chorus of obscenities, they began ranting about ice. Zipping open our bags, the rest of us suddenly came to the same realization. Someone had fiendishly filled our sleeping bags with ice cubes. Nothing so villainous had ever happened to us before. Revenge was due. We quickly changed into whatever dry clothes we could recover. Our mission was clear and simple. The suspected culprits must be hunted down.

With the rain still falling, we marched toward the far end of the campground in search of the site number given to us by the beach babes. During our crusade, we conspired on how to get even. Upon spotting the number, we stomped into the site and banged on the camp trailer door. Surprisingly, an elderly couple responded to the commotion. Clearly, deceptive information had duped us. Embarrassed and apologetic, we slogged away to continue our vigilante venture. Fortunately, the rain subsided. Unfortunately, there were more than two hundred sites in the huge campground and the she-devils were nowhere to be found.

Though we were not permanently washed up as studs on this woeful weekend, a lesson in reality had soaked in. Perhaps we were not quite ready to be really cool studs yet. For now, our hopes and dreams would remain on ice. In the meantime, we had to warm up to the idea of chilling out. If only the good sisters of Saint Joe's had fully prepared us for this unexpected cold front our spirits might never have been so dampened. Maybe, just maybe, a little public education was all that we needed.

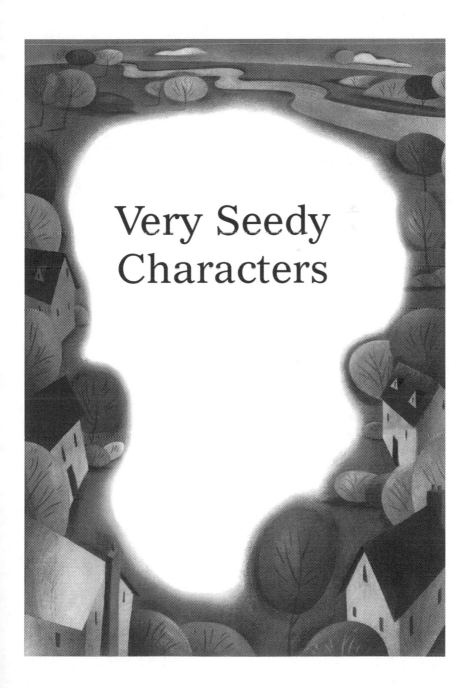

Very Seedy Characters

Once upon a town untangled, young rogues gathered together for mentoring by their illicit elders. What they were about to engender and execute would lead to a remorseful, rotten, and pathetic ending. Nonetheless, these rogues persevered and paid the price by tasting the seedy side of life. Never would they hunger for the same again.

Call it a rite of passage. Call it a cultural crusade. Most of all, call it traditional peer-pressure pranks. But please, never refer to this as organized crime. Oh sure, it does involve some organizational effort. And yes, borderline criminal activity conspires of sorts. However, let's be honest. This is entrapment blistered by the collusion of law enforcement and a syndicate known as Piggly Wiggly.

Like it or not, there truly is a dark side to each of us. During the teenage years, it is termed juvenile delinquency. Among most youth, this means either suppressing or succumbing to deep-rooted primal temptations. Weak or strong, breakdowns loom because something has to give. When that occurs, which was generally inevitable in my hometown, it is easy to understand how one can haplessly become a homegrown melon felon.

In this opportune neck of the woods, the temptations were far too great, the challenges so noble, and the watermelons just right for picking. The culmination occurred near my hometown's northern outskirts. As midsummer approached each year, the pretentious Piggly Wiggly proceeded to bait its trap. Layers upon layers of the forbidden fruit were stacked outside the grocery store in broad daylight. Four to five deep, these juicy juggernauts formed a green barricade from the store's entryway to the back loading dock.

Now that my friends and I were well entrenched into high school, our predecessors finally shared the true secret of life. To become a real man, you must pillage and plunder the fruit of the "Pig." These clandestine quests were made even more challenging due to this loony labeled grocery being just across the road from the county jail. Under the cover of darkness, however, anything was possible in this midsummer night's dream.

Although appearing young and innocent, my gang of cohorts was already experienced in covert operations. This savvy clan oftentimes included the police chief's son. We had become routinely accomplished at scaling the walls of the middle school, creeping across the lower rooftop, and crawling through the unlocked window of the teacher's lounge. This then provided open access for midnight carousing while cloaked in obscurity. Vandalism was never an aim of our escapades. This was strictly an expedition to expose the mysteries of an archaic three-story teen penitentiary. Once the students are dismissed, all teachers and staff depart, and the janitors head home after locking the doors. Burning within us was the unrelenting question: does anyone or anything remain behind? Answers must be found.

Sometimes we skulked into the cafeteria only to be repulsed by the permanent aroma of decomposing leftovers and overly applied disinfectant. At other times, we darted about in the gym while playing imaginary basketball games. Mostly however, we prowled the cavernous corridors where every footstep seemed amplified by the tile floors, reverberated off the metal lockers, and then echoed from a distance as if someone else was stalking us. Being skittish of our own sounds and shadows resulted in a frenzied stampede to the nearest exit.

As a point of reference, this is the same gang that somehow acquired possession of a master key to every room in the parochial grade school. However, no connections or conclusions should be made in regard to any missing items such as ice cream bars from the school freezer or a case of Jolly Good soda from the adjacent storage pantry. Perhaps it would be remiss not to also mention the "munch a bunch" expeditions to that small building near the Black Death Cemetery. For the record, I, for one, never actively participated in sneaking through the garage window of the regional Frito-Lay salesman, who routinely left his delivery truck unlocked and fully loaded. There may be a slight possibility, however, that I consumed some of the evidence collected by others.

Another option for dereliction involved trekking to a secluded orchard on the southeast edge of town where the owner left his old car unlocked and gassed up. With keys in its ignition, this opportunity served as a well-established temptation for limited excursions. Upon the intimidating acquisition of a German shepherd to guard the orchards, the joyriding ceased immediately. Our only other deviant alternative was to seek out ancient outhouses and topple them asunder. However, this rabble-rousing dissipated as remaining upright outhouses became few and far between. If any were to be found, they were usually pilfered for placement atop the annual high school homecoming bonfire. This honorable sacrifice seemed much more civilized than that of my father's generation, which involved depositing the hijacked wooden privy at a main street intersection, setting it ablaze, and then hiding out as the panicked police arrived.

As some traditions began to fade, one remained intact and would not be denied. Late on an August dog day of heat and humidity, my friends and I cast aside the doldrums and prepared for this challenge. Gathering behind the Masonic Temple, we met with our upper-class mentors to absorb their wisdom of wanderlust. Instructed by these wisenheimers, we divided into two groups. One was tasked with incendiary diversions, while the other would stalk incognito through the farm fields behind Piggly Wiggly. Once in position, our precision maneuvers would commence.

These ensuing shenanigans depicted a hometown hullabaloo well known by local authorities and this grocer. To thwart any late night marauding, one of the police officers would routinely station himself and his patrol car near the store's rear loading dock. From this vantage point, he could easily survey the melons as they glowed under the parking lot lights. Thanks to expert guidance, however, we had planned for this obstacle. As our merry band of stalkers approached the back side of the store, the diversion team was already in place to undergo strategic operations. Their job was to activate fireworks in the nearby parking lot of the Lutheran church. As an additional diversionary tactic, cherry bombs with delayed fuses had been planted in garbage cans several blocks away. This served to attract the attention of any police in the proximity, who would then pursue the pyromaniacs. Left unguarded, the prized produce would now be ripe for the picking.

As one of the stalkers, I saw this caper not only as a challenge, but also an opportunity for stardom. My personal goal was to snatch not just any melon, but bag the biggest trophy of all. Relying on the rationale of my advanced adolescent intellect, the bigger the melon, the greater the spoils. Little did I know about the profound nature of such prophecy. Following the instructions of our mentors, we silently crept along the farm fields that bordered the boundaries on the back side of the store. Upon arriving and peering through the fence line underbrush, we sighted Officer Tiny sitting comfortably in his cruiser. Undaunted and according to plan, we waited patiently for the fireworks to begin. As an arsenal of bottle rockets, M-80s, aerial bombs, firecrackers, and cherry bombs suddenly exploded down the street, Officer Tiny stormed out of the parking lot in hot pursuit. Right on cue, we jumped the fence and dashed madly for the melons. In keeping with my personal goal, I searched frantically for a behemoth. Upon finding the prize, I joined my comrades in sprinting back to the fence line.

With arms wrapped tightly around our melons, we could not contain our emotions or our presence while jogging across the recently cropped hayfield. Each of us seemed possessed by uncontrollable laughter. The booty had been claimed, and now it was time to celebrate. Suddenly however, spotlights shot beams across the field and created an illuminating dragnet. No matter how fast we ran, the spotlights followed. A loudspeaker echoed out a warning for us to stop, yet we had no intention of slowing down or heeding the command. To speed up, everyone around me started tossing their treasure. I nearly tripped over several melons as I continued to clutch mine and run for my life. The only thought in my mind at this time was to hang on and fly like the wind until reuniting at the rendezvous point behind the Masonic Temple.

As we reached the end of the field, the gang split off in different directions. Watching the spotlights and hearing sirens, I chose the quickest course away from the mayhem. Running through backyards while dodging clotheslines and chained dogs, the sweat poured off me on this solo flight to the Masonic Temple. With arms throbbing from a headlock on the melon, routine rests were needed before losing my grip. Finally, by the grace of adrenaline, I staggered to the rendezvous point. As the last to arrive, jubilation began upon discovering that I was the only one to return with a watermelon. It was now time to celebrate, munch down the melon, and savor this conquest. And so we did, yet with unsavory results.

Biggest is not always better when it comes to watermelons. Oversized can translate to overripe. As each of us bit into our seed-laden slices, moans and groans were followed by a resounding gagging in the midnight air. This melon was rotten to the core. My friends were not just spitting seeds, they were spitting up. This booty was a blunder rather than a plunder. All my sweat, toil, and tears left me with a bad taste in my mouth. In contemplating this rite of passage, I earned an unexpected education. Sometimes in learning lessons and getting a taste of life, you've just got to sink your teeth into it and swallow a little pride. Better yet, never bite off more than you can chew or pig out on easy pickings.

Cliché as all this may sound, it is nothing more than fruitful advice for treatment of "melon choly." Any remorse on my part was eradicated by the thought that I forthrightly removed a morbid melon from the pile of perfectly good produce. As such, there is certainly no need for penance and perhaps, it is the "Pig" who truly owes me a debt of gratitude.

As a closing disclaimer, do not interpret any of the previous passages as a promotion for outlaw activity. Mild mannered mischief should never be confused with hard-core crime. Nefarious young knuckleheads do not necessarily evolve into vandals or lifelong villains. Know that without a little mayhem in every Mayberry, small towns like mine might surely decease from boredom and blahs. Therefore, deal with the denial and understand that a prankster resides within each of us. Letting it fester would surely be the real crime. Just outgrow it and get through it as early as possible. And of course, never ever get caught.

Should all this sound as if my friends and I lacked scruples, let it be known that we never engaged in demeaning endeavors like snipe hunts. No cow-tippers or sign-swipers were part of this gang. Not one of us ever lifted an eight-track player or anything else from anyone's car. And although we may have been party to a few smashed pumpkins and toilet paper adorned trees, no bombardment of eggs got included in these escapades.

To add a footnote, our incidental pilfering pales in comparison to that of a resident harness maker who distinguished himself as the region's most notorious horse thief. During the late 1800s, a Civil War veteran named Agrelius moved to this area and set up a leatherworks shop. In reality, it was a convenient front for is true vocation of stealing horses. Well liked by his rural neighbors, he entertained them as a storyteller and accomplished ventriloquist.

Oftentimes, Argelius would disappear for weeks while abducting horses from nearby states. He became extremely skilled at dying horses to change their colors and markings. Pursued by the local Anti-Horsethief Association, he was arrested in 1877, 1883, 1892, and 1903 but usually received light sentences due to his ability to challenge the courts on technicalities or establish a reasonable doubt. Well into his seventies, Argelius's final bust occurred in 1904 when an extensive horse-stealing operation was traced to a cave near the state line.

It's hard to believe such ruthlessness being perpetrated by the son of a Swedish clergyman. If the clock was turned ahead one hundred years and more, can you imagine what kind of horsing around this culprit would have initiated at the nearest Piggly Wiggly? No matter the century and no matter the place, never is there a shortage of seedy characters.

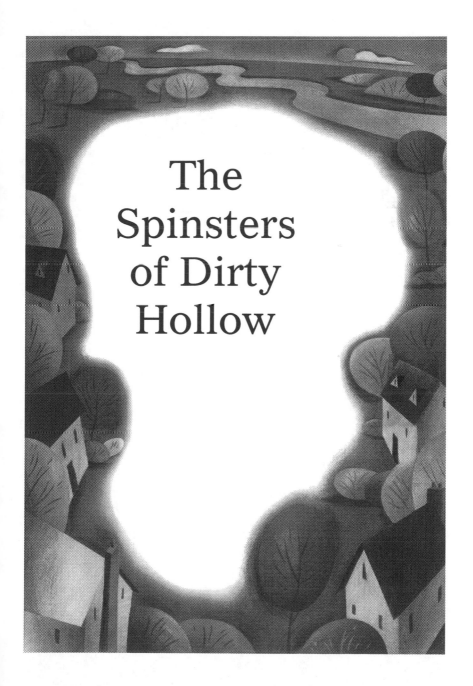

The
Spinsters
of Dirty
Hollow

Once upon a town untangled, steaming trains rolled through it, cryptic caverns snaked beneath it, frumpy hobos hung around it, and from the very midst of it, a cherished lake was spirited away. In the meantime, the legend of two intriguing sisters burgeoned in a place called Dirty Hollow. It is a legacy to be remembered.

Even though its moniker has been long abandoned, Dirty Hollow really exists. Most of the locals have only a vague idea of where it is. Even the old timers strain to recollect what they know about this boundary area that divided the high-life neighborhoods from the poor side of town. In reality, Dirty Hollow would only be deemed a small part of a small place, nothing of significance. Then again, it was home sweet home to the Spinster sisters.

Dirty Hollow begins near the limestone opera house and cheese depot. It then runs east following a tiny spring that flows past an ancient slag furnace, power plant, horse stables, feed mill, and lumber yard. This is the same spring that once fed into a fashionable swimming hole known as Crystal Lake. Dastardly, the lake was pirated. It disappeared along with the boat piers, band pavilion, concession stand, and merry-go-round. Vanquished as well was the gigantic water slide. This shoreline venue had been built and donated by the village wagonwright, who also utilized the lake for a thriving ice delivery business. Those who know little about Dirty Hollow recall even less about this mysterious lake. It vanished one day when the labyrinth of lead ore mines beneath its underbelly caved in and drained the lake dry. The exact same thing happened to another lake in a nearby town.

Although the lake is forever gone, a tiny spring continues to trickle through Dirty Hollow. Adjacent to its path are the modest homes that were built for the miners and other laborers who congregated here. Just like the lake that is bygone, so too are the coal yards and railroad depot responsible for the naming of Dirty Hollow. The railway that progressed through Dirty Hollow haled at its west end where an innovative round house reversed the train engines. The result of this maneuver created inversions of belched black smoke while idling trains unloaded their cargos. Thus, both the label and legacy of Dirty Hollow were derived from the heaving iron horses.

Some claim that the name Dirty Hollow actually stems from the swampy bottomlands of this valley. In its early days, an expansive trestle traversed this area to accommodate both the trains and local kids who utilized this wooden structure as a massive set of monkey bars. Because the major focus of Dirty Hollow was the railway and rail yards, it also served as part-time residence to many hobos. During the Depression era, this locale took on the added nickname of Hobo Jungle. Many of these vagrants pandered soup bones from the nearby meat market or handouts from area homes. It became common knowledge among them as to who sympathized with their situations. Clustered around rail yard campfires, these vagabonds also spent considerable time filtering Sterno and other fuels through bread slices to satisfy their liquid cravings.

Over the years, Dirty Hollow lost its charm as the railroad industry dwindled. All the iron rails and creosote timbers that shouldered the trains were dismantled into memories. Both local depots disappeared. The north/south route, once used by my paternal grandfather to commute by handcar to his teaching job in a nearby town, was reclaimed by farm fields and side roads. The east/west line converted to a trendy bicycle trail that passes through the farmlands of my sister, maternal grandfather, and uncles. As a young boy, this is the railroad section where I collected curious rocks and rusted railroad spikes. And of course, there were always those tempting times when a penny had to be placed on the iron rails for reshaping by the next passing train. It just seemed like the radical thing to do.

As railroading waned, so too did the three roadhouses of Dirty Hollow, including one known as the Rough and Ready. The signature opera house is gone as well after surviving more than 150 years as an entertainment center, sports arena, creamery, cigar factory, car dealership, and blacksmith shop. Before it was demolished to make way for an expanded gas station, a neighbor used the space to store his collection of horse buggies and carriages.

However, the legacy of Dirty Hollow does not end here. Most of its renowned residents dwelt at the far eastern reaches of Dirty Hollow. A weather-beaten ramshackle cabin of the mining era was home to the Spinster sisters. Where they came from or how they got here endured as a mystery. No power lines, water lines, or telephone lines connected this shelter to the outside world. The only signs of life within were gray hazy wisps rising from the cabin's rooftop smokestack. Behind this abode was an outhouse, far too sacred for any high school revelers to swipe for the annual homecoming bonfire. Alongside this homestead, the valley spring trickled after leaching through the upstream dormant mines and tailings. This spring served as the Spinsters' main water supply. Some surmise the noxious nature of this water intoxicated the character of these siblings.

The tiny parcel they occupied was by no means prime real estate. To the east, there stood the remains of an aging lead ore smelter. On the hill above the Spinsters' home was the East Side Cemetery. Behind them, the town dump sprawled with its aromatic ambiance. Over time, it seemed as if both the dump and cemetery were destined to converge and become one continuous burial ground surrounding these sisters. Residing in the midst of all this only enhanced their notoriety.

Small towns are not always a good fit for big-time celebrities. Therefore, you make do with those around you. Without a doubt, the Spinsters were community icons and the town's version of celebrity status. Just the mere sighting of these two ladies was cause for pause. In another era, they may have been tagged with the slang labels of bent hairpins or hagmeyers. Their attire and antics became legendary among the local wags. As they sauntered about this town, their rigid formation was always the same. One sister took the lead while the other followed directly behind. They never departed from this single file configuration. Tall and lanky, the Spinster sisters routinely dressed as if an endless cold spell had set in. They were cocooned in long overcoats, heavyweight slacks, and tightly knotted head scarves. Their feet were covered in peasant-like shoes known as half boots. Only in the heat of the summer would they vary from this fully clad attire. They shunned any gala color or glimmer as if to camouflage themselves with the dreary look of an overcast midwinter day

The complexions of the Spinsters' faces were weathered gray and etched by the decades. It was incredibly difficult to guess their ages. Always painted old, no one could ever recall them as young. Like the hunchback clerk who worked forever at the downtown bakery and the stone-faced manager guarding the theater entryway, the Spinsters seemed like never-changing local figures frozen in time.

Whenever these sisters marched about, their eyes were cast downward, expressions sullen, and demeanor dispirited. They shadowed about like apparitions locked into a somber pattern and personality from which there was no escape. As such, many considered the Spinsters just plain spooky. Little was ever said by this tandem because little was ever said to them. One ongoing rumor claimed they spoke a language of gibberish that was theirs alone. To avoid greetings or making eye contact, some concerned citizens would step off the sidewalks as the siblings approached. Many townies were too mystified and afraid of a close encounter. Most kids found this duo quite bashfully bewildering.

Whenever the Spinsters were out and about, their paths were ritually plotted routes to the grocery store for food or the hospital where they worked. They rarely ventured elsewhere. However, that did not mean there were no delays along the way. On hot summer afternoons, the sisters often stopped to rest at the shaded entrance to the county courthouse. Ascending the steps, they would then lie prone on the cool concrete ledges that fronted the judicial building. Although this was not a main street sight favored by the town's Chamber of Commerce, no city official dared to disrupt this routine.

One day, farther down the block and directly in front of the senior center, a Spinster sister decided to grab onto the lamp post and swing about as if it were a maypole. This became a major distraction to the cribbage cronies and other elder gamers at the center. It also fueled the gossiping gadabouts for a considerable time. Like all the antics of the sisters, their actions remained harmless. So what if they were often observed buying feline food at the grocery store and yet had no cats? Never mind the rumor that alleged one sister chased the other with a huge meat cleaver during a work dispute at the hospital kitchen. As for the frequent sightings of these women skulking about in the Eastside Cemetery, bear in mind that crossing through this property represented a logical shortcut from their house to the hospital.

It must be noted that the Spinster sisters were not the original odd couple to roam these parts. In 1849, a Cornish couple took up residence in the area as farmers. Husband Frederick stood at seven foot four and his wife Jane was just over seven feet; it did not take long for local folk to notice them. These two goliaths had previously performed with General Tom Thumb in P.T. Barnum's traveling show. Also working also as a teamster, the 370-pound farmer with size twenty-one shoes reputedly could pick up an eighty-pound chunk of lead with one hand, carry fence rails by the bundle, and lift a four hundred-pound whiskey barrel with his fingertips. A circus poster featured him hoisting a Shetland pony. During this international vocation, Frederick somehow became accused of being a foreign spy. Other rumors pegged him as a hit man. Changing his surname to a Scottish identity raised suspicions as well. When he died at middle-age and under mysterious circumstances, speculation escalated even more about the life and death of this Cornish Hercules.

Later in this same era, a revelation overcame a town attorney, who for reasons unknown, suddenly ended his law practice. He also swore off all alcohol and tobacco, pledged a vow of poverty, became a vegetarian, began sporting a lengthy white beard, and spent most of his remaining days communing with the deceased in the cemetery. He thus earned the title of "Archibald the Hermit." Upon his death in December 1926, the eighty-one-year-old recluse was found to have more than $250,000 in assets. To each of his closest relatives, he willed $5 each. The remainder of his fortune went to a stranger that he met at a park bench. Due to his notoriety, Archibald's obituary became a feature article in the state's largest newspaper.

Years later, during my upbringing in this humble town, the Spinsters starred as an everyday drama. Although appearing drab and dreary, this conspicuous pair made everyone else just ordinary and obscure. Without the Spinsters, the community would never have been the same. That is especially true for the youthful gawkers who marveled at these sisters and created many of the embellished stories surrounding them.

Describing the Spinsters' home as a shanty is no exaggeration. Unpainted and unadorned, many speculated as to the worldly possessions hidden inside. No one ever dared set foot on this property or peer through its windows. Boneheads training to be juvenile delinquents often targeted the Spinsters. As typical down-home rednecks taking part in pea-brained escapades, teenagers would often drive by the sisters' house to sling obscenities and water balloons. Based more on monotony than meanness, sometimes the misguided mayhem spiraled out of control.

It was inevitable that a confrontation would ensue at the Spinsters' home. With Halloween fast approaching, someone hatched the cockamamie and compelling idea to Trick or Treat at this peculiar place. The conspiracy was simple and only required the ritual of knocking on the door to request a treat. However, a bit of a twist was added. One of the passengers in a car of crazy teens had purchased a President Nixon mask from what was proudly promoted as the "World's Longest Ben Franklin" store. A decision was quickly made. Whoever ventured forth to the Spinsters' house must do so while wearing this dime-store mask and proclaiming the infamous quote, "I am not a crook."

As Halloween arrived, so too did a crammed car to the far edge of Dirty Hollow. The stage was now set for one brave and bold soul to step out, secure the mask, and then march forward with a treat bag in hand. The only remaining element was to establish who that might be. Among the teenage entourage was a kid named Pete. He was the youngest of this gang and suffered from an identity crisis. Pete was not considered an athlete, scholar, class clown, dirtbag, geek, nerd, hick, dunce, or anything else. He was simply Pete and just average at everything.

Pete knew he lacked any kind of reputation and resented this distinction. Poised at the threshold to Dirty Hollow's most eminent landmark, he realized that the opportunity of a lifetime now dawned before him. This masquerade would create an impression unparalleled among his peers.

No one contested Pete's motion to volunteer for this mission. As he stepped from the car and into the darkness, the driver handed Pete a flashlight. With the car lights turned off, the flashlight was his only means of guidance. Proceeding forward, Pete soon found himself stumbling through the bramble surrounding the Spinster's house. No sounds or lights emitted from this dwelling. Despite the aid of the flashlight, Pete was impaired by the unfamiliar setting and the mask that partially obscured his vision.

Sitting in silence, Pete's friends strained to watch his progress toward the front porch. As Pete stepped on to the wooden entryway, its floorboards creaked loudly. Suddenly, the night air shattered as the shadowy figure of Pete shouted out, "I am not a crook!" Before he could complete a repeat of this historic quote, Pete stopped in midsentence and wailed a terrorizing scream. As his friends peered in to the gloom, all they could see was a flashlight waving madly about. Whatever Pete was yelling could not be deciphered. To the gang's amazement, both Pete's voice and the flashlight beam mysteriously faded. When one of the car passengers got nervous and shrieked something about an approaching Spinster, the car's driver panicked. Within seconds, the engine roared and tires squealed as Pete's cowardly comrades raced away. Pete was marooned.

Pete somehow survived the ordeal and eventually made it back to his home. Shortly thereafter, his deserting friends stopped by to check on him. They wanted to know what happened and what Pete had seen. Pete refused to share any details. His only comment was to say that if his friends had remained behind to help him, they too would know what he now knows. The car's driver tried to apologize for the abrupt departure by explaining that he had recently gotten into trouble and could not afford to get caught again. Pete rejected the apology and all further attempts to solicit information relating to this nightmarish event. Although word quickly spread about the Halloween caper, Pete continued steadfast on the secrecy of his audacious encounter. In doing so, both Pete's reputation and that of the Spinsters flourished.

Living near the town's outskirts, these biddies were apart from the community and yet a part of it as well. Every town has its old maids, often miscast as witches, hags, and harpy loners, yet never mistaken as harlots or hussies. Prejudiced by countenance and conduct, they are the books judged by their covers. No one bothers to read the chapters or between the lines. Knowing the whole story would simply mitigate the fables we want to believe.

Without a doubt, the mystique of Dirty Hollow owes much to these sisters. Most townspeople were unaware there were actually three Spinsters christened Rose, Viola, and Fern. Which names belonged to which sister remains a mystery, along with the unknown residence of the third sister. Despite their faded blossom facades, the Spinsters were perennial wildflowers in the local landscape. Like a dried floral arrangement, what these sisters lacked in color, they made up for in contrast and character. Not appraised as pillars of society, community leaders, or influential business persons, nonetheless, the Spinsters contributed just the same. What they gave us were memories, intrigue, and another layer to the town's legacy. In this hometown, that was more than enough to enrich our lives.

Gone forever, the rickety shack of this entrancing twosome no longer exists. Condemned by the local bureaucrats, this landmark of times past was torn down after the Spinster sisters were uprooted to another residence. Within the rubble that remained of their razed shanty, a curious object was found wedged in the crawl space beneath the floor boards. Made of molded plastic, discolored and cracked, it outlandishly resembled the profile of Richard Milhous Nixon. Imagine that—for Pete's sake.

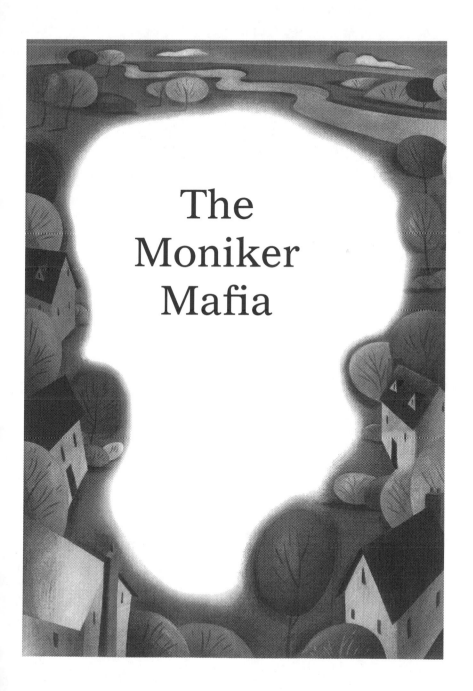

The Moniker Mafia

Once upon a town untangled, an identity crisis ran amuck. A game to name was the name of this game. Participation was an edict rather than an option. Worse yet, this perilous game often transformed into a vexing curse. For some, the curse had a short life span. For the less fortunate, it persisted as never ending. Although unfair and oftentimes nasty, it remained a lingering reality.

Beware of this curse for its power has no equal. It manifests everywhere, yet is more prevalent in familiar places. Without warning, the curse can strike at any time. Like a hideous beast, this horrid phenomenon raises its ugly head from an evil abyss while sometimes disguised as fondness or affection. More often than not, it transpires into the cruelest of cruel fates. The curse is not a random act but rather the cold calculated undertaking of an extremist faction known despicably as the Moniker Mafia.

This malicious cult thrives on name-tag terrorism. Without conscience or morals, the Moniker Mafia attacks innocent victims and brands them for life. These assassins of personal identity are the unsanctified creators of nicknames. From their ruthless and sinister executions, none of us can hide.

The curse of the Moniker Mafia had a stronghold on my hometown. It pillaged and plundered with reckless abandon. No one was safe, and nothing was sacred. The only granting of protection came to those bearing common names such as Jones, Smith, Murphy, or Anderson. As a result, they were naturally dubbed Jonesy, Smitty, Murf, or Andy. Others however, were less fortunate. Without recourse, you could find yourself christened according to rhyming schemes, reconfigured pronunciations, physical attributes, reputations, or nicknames absolutely unrelated to anything about you.

To exemplify the wrath of the Moniker Mafia, one hometown victim's surname was often mispronounced as "urine." He thus became commonly known as Piss. Other examples were not so extreme. Rooster was named for his red hair, Keg for his size and stature, Injun based on a claim of Native American ancestry,

Professor based on his thick glasses, and Bat because the mafia viewed his high-arching eyebrows as akin to that of a vampire.

No compassion existed in this name game. Far too many labels lacked any rationale such as Skunk, Warthog, Hound Dog, Mole, Muskrat, Squirrel, Bearcat, and Moon Duck. Added to this zoo crew were Goose, Pig, Tuna, Cubby, Bird, and Bunny, all due to links with their real names. Seems to me, a Mouse existed as well. The mafia also took it upon itself to single out unique characteristics. A visually impaired student tagged Radar had to endure shouts of "beep, beep, beep" whenever he played basketball and attempted a shot. Tight curly hair translated to Brillo for another student. The school's only known gay person gained notoriety as Sugar Bear. Those who attended the special education programs in room B5 earned distinction as B-fivers.

Just to name a few, my fellow classmates included Chi-town, Frick, Hatter, Juice, Raz, Rock, Snotter, Squeeny, Strivey, Stud, Tweet, and Who. There were guys called Butt, Cess, Dong, Muey, Parker, and Pickle for reasons known and unknown. One kid was branded with the surname of the notorious Spinsters. My conference track rival was a kid I knew only as Stick. And of course, just down the road was my neighbor Salami. All of this made reunions quite awkward when five to ten years later you could not always recall their real names.

Teachers served as perfect targets for the Moniker Mafia. To the best of my recollection, these included Chrome Dome, Cookie Man, Fossil Face, Freddy Bear, Wild Bill, Henny Penny, and Prune Face. Although this juvenile jargon began as attempts to poke fun at these educators, their nicknames often evolved into labels of fondness rather than foolishness. Even coaches made it into the alias arena. Mention Coach Weenie and everyone knew just who you meant. After winning the state basketball tournament, this comical christening turned to celebrity status. It was much better to be a winning Weenie than a losing one. Without any mafia assistance, a biology teacher was addressed as Mister Woods and a wrestling coach as Mister Wildman. Coincidentally, these were their real names.

Nicknames were not always adversarial in nature. An ongoing shoulder injury and sling earned one athlete the title of Wing. Another was called Lumpy, which this big dude seemed to accept as suitable. His teammate carried the tag of Tater. Chocolate's nickname described his brunette complexion. Had he not favored this moniker, at six foot seven, he could have imposed considerable influence. Instead, this popular nickname resulted in a school cheer using the Nestles' advertising jingle.

At times, the Moniker Mafia was less cruel and chose to assign nicknames that sounded somewhat similar to one's actual name. This resulted in Arnie, Bucko, Clutch, Hambone, Harley, Enertube, Ike, Munster, Lefty, Oly, Ozark, Rodey, Rosey, Tread, Witty, and Zeke. Even this practice got out of control at times. One of my best friends began as Whitey, evolved into Weavey, then Lidey, then Laudy, then Lima, and finally Clyde. Some never knew that his given name was Steve. His freckled brother Jim began as Red and eventually changed to Jagger. So profound was this mafia that actual names became forgotten and phone listings useless. You had to scratch your head and strain the brain just to recall birth names.

Perhaps the most vulnerable victims of the Moniker Mafia were the young ladies of questionable reputations or extraordinary physiques. For them, the mafia rose to elevated heights of meanness. Those who had the misfortune to fit into this category were fortunate if they did not have a surname that rhymed with any kind of derogatory term. For example, a name of Gilmore or Bagley could easily transition to Gilwhore or Skagley. Femininity also factored into this formula. Being supersized could foster a Mama Moose or Baby Huey identity. Misbehave and you could become a Loosey. Some of these nasty names diminished with time while others remained haplessly entrenched.

In a neighboring town, there was a family name that not even the mafia could change or alter. It was so descriptive in nature that instead of vocabulary, body language was used to articulate this moniker. With the surname of Sniff, a gesture of nasal inhaling was used in reference to this individual. Then again, I once met a man whose last name was Crapper. Perhaps a nickname might have improved upon on his surname.

Well established, the Moniker Mafia existed for many generations before me. My father had friends designated Toad, Digger, Jiggs, Speed, Happy, Smiley, Duke, Moon, Butch, Bud, Stretch, and Baldy. When help was needed, he contacted Gibby for electrical work, Tuffy for plumbing, and Pony for carpentry. One local police officer was ardently referred to as Tiny, even though his humungous stature required routine replacement of the patrol car seat springs. Hometown hooligans loved this character. Whenever he stepped out of his cruiser, this rotund cop was not about to run down anyone.

Others in town came to be known as Chicken Man, Ducky, Deerskin, Big John, Farmer, Cowboy, Corky, Gussy, Punkin' Head, Ghouly, Sunny, and Snuffy Smith. Not to be remiss, I must also include Woody the snake man. He wandered about the nearby bluffs and collected resident rattlers during the five dollar bounty era. Digging into this area's past unearths names such as River Rat Fred, Archibald the Hermit, Madam Louise, Iron Lena, Badger Bill, Apple Jack, Scotch Giant, Popcorn George, and the Hiding Kickapoo.

By no means did the Moniker Mafia lack in divinity. Even the most pious were touched by its influence. Non-Catholics carried the label of Publics. In response, Catholics became known as Catlickers, Mackerel Snappers, and Fish Eaters. Regardless of denomination, those most fervent became the Holy Rollers, God Squad, and Jesus Freaks. Anyone who came knocking at your front door formally clad and toting a Bible was relegated a Stormin' Mormon. The isolated Amish of this region earned the distinction of Plowboys. For whatever reason, the local Wiccan congregation was spared any additional designation.

During the 1970s, truckers and other drivers attempted to circumvent the Moniker Mafia by creating the CB craze. By adding citizens band radios to everything that moved, the art of nicknaming became self-inflicted. People arbitrarily identified themselves by the handle of choice. A friend of mine, who wanted an innocent and non-provocative handle, dubbed himself Simple

Christian. This handle did not last long as he soon found himself flooded with calls from a deluge of motoring ministers and evangelists. As a lesson learned, never mess with rhetoric that attempts to bypass the mafia's realm.

Sometimes the mafia's deplorable curse can even become a career when nicknames evolve into stage names. My buddies and I experienced this phenomenon on our first trip to the state fair. Just as we entered the midway, a carnival barker beckoned us to witness the most bizarre and breathtaking wonders of the living world. After paying the entrance fee, we soon found ourselves encountering the performer Popeye. He possessed the ability to pop his real right eye completely out of its socket and let it dangle for audience approval. Next, we encountered the Alligator Lady born with reptilian skin and the Lobster Man whose hands resembled huge crustacean claws. Other oddball characters followed as well. This of course was a full-fledged show where eccentricities were exploited. In these despicable displays, human deformities translated into commercial labels. Although I believed that this carnival custom had been banished, a recent regional fair advertised the Human Tripod, a woman born with one leg and two long arms.

Following high school graduation, I recognized my opportunity to flee this name game and avert its curse. The esteemed halls of higher education now beckoned as a civilized refuge from the malarkey of a small town. What I encountered instead was a rude awakening. Shortly after moving into my university dorm room, I met Igor from next door. His nickname stemmed from the removal of knee cartilage in each leg. As a result, he ambled about in an Igor-like fashion. Although his legs suffered from past football injuries, he retained massive upper body muscles and took advantage of his Herculean strength. Igor randomly wandered into dorm rooms and greeted any inhabitant with a breathtaking bear hug until there was a cry for mercy. On occasion, Igor would tie up the captive with a stretched telephone cord and exit the room.

You learned to tolerate such tenacity when your neighbor is titled Igor and has a girlfriend named Killer.

A cast of characters was never lacking in this student residence. Long-haired Whitey spent his entire freshman year toking joints and pounding on his bass guitar. Sky High Jerry rarely left his room because his recreational resources were far more potent than Whitey's. Iguana resided toward the opposite end of the hall. He was aptly christened due to his lanky six foot six frame and sparse 150 pound physique. Interspersed throughout the rest of the dorm were Big Stick, Bilbo, Chopper, Clouds, Fish, Fly, Newt, Scoogs, Sea Hag, Shoe, Soosh, Space Captain, Stork, and Tee. Hounder, Warthog, and Diver, from my hometown, lived in the dorm as well.

Eventually, I moved off campus to live with Little Joe and Pup. My college cohort Mutley, resembled a bespectacled version of the character Shaggy in *Scooby Doo*. Both of us were campus Hobbits. During a summer college break, Mutley and I worked at a wilderness camp for Boy Scouts and inner-city kids. Mutley entertained the campers by jumping through the enormous bonfire event that was held weekly. Unfortunately, Mutley miscalculated his steps one evening and had to be rescued from the burning embers. Perhaps he should have been named Sparky like a friend of mine, who earned his moniker while playing with matches as a young boy and igniting his family's garage. After college, Mutley signed on as a research scientist at Kodak, which I'm pretty sure is a safe haven from bonfires.

Just when coming to terms with this collegiate version of the Moniker Mafia, I met Gorilla in a rousing manner. Gorilla started as tight end for the university's football team. However, my personal introduction to him was on the basketball court. Gorilla was a member of the opposing intramural team. At first sight, I easily understood his moniker. Cro Magnum or Neanderthal would have fit as well. He was enormous with dark hair protruding from every visible part of his body. With no apparent neck, a rectangular jaw, flattened nose, and one continuous eyebrow, this goliath was imposing. Early into the game, I hit two quick outside shots. When the time was ripe for my third attempt, Gorilla had other plans. As I went up with the ball, this goon greeted me with a right uppercut to the jaw. Lying dazed on the court floor and bleeding, I looked up to see the referee staring at me. When I asked about calling a foul, he glanced toward Gorilla, rolled his eyes, and walked away. At this moment, I became my own mafia with all kinds of labels for this referee. Wimp, Wuss, and Bozo are the only ones I can discretely mention.

Anyone growing up in any small town must accept the reality that nicknames are a way of life. They stem from both monotony and familiarity. Little is sacred when it comes to the voodoo vocabulary of a name game. It cannot be prevented because no one knows where it begins. If someone did find out, there might surely be considerable consequences and regrets. Then again, this would mean a risky intrusion into the territory of the Moniker Mafia.

Bear in mind, the Moniker Mafia infiltrates everyone's hometown. A retreat or escape might lead to a possible reprieve. Then again, there is always the chance of ending up in a place where you establish close ties with the likes of an Igor. Even worse, you may encounter someone named Gorilla going ape on you. Just be wary when giving it your best shot.

Stalked by a Ghost

Once upon a town untangled, a haunting endeavored and never ended. Somewhere out there, along fence lines and woodlots, atop rolling hills, and skittishly hidden in dark hollows, a spirit lives on. Most often it remains peaceful, yet there are times of restlessness when the encounters turn eerie, outlandish, and downright unforgettable. This is simply a stark and ghoulish reality in my neck of the woods.

Let this spirited tale unfold by stating that it truly is a ghost story. The main character is by no means a Casper the Friendly Ghost, a head-hurling Ichabod Crane, the Ghost of Christmas Past, or a biblical Holy Ghost. It is, however, a decent sort of spook credited with everything that cannot be explained around here. For more than a century and a half, this intriguing entity has made its presence well known to the locals. Sometimes it is a shadowy figure, motionless and forlorn in the distant roadway. Other times, it has manifested as a horse, dog, or misshapen medium. As such, this spector may very well be a changeling, shape-shifter, or what Native Americans call the Skinwalker. Possibly it is the wandering spirit of the great chief Blackhawk, hunted down and driven from his homeland by a hell-bent militia that included a volunteer named Abe Lincoln. Several sightings proclaim it to be a pale woman dressed in white and riding a goat—somewhat reminiscent of the storied Irish Banchee. Others use the name Gloommadoom n reference to the shady faceless character sneaking about. It may even be the unhappy soul of an internationally renowned architect whose local castle got set ablaze while his mistress was being hacked to death by the butler. Perhaps it is not one but many ghosts from times and places where countless strange events have transpired.

Ever since the territorial governor of 1844 laid claim to being a medium, this region has continued its legacy of spiritualism. On a visit to Washington, D.C., this politician often conducted séances that involved calling upon the spirit of a former senate colleague. According to a witnessed account, one of these séances resulted in a massive table dancing about the room. When the movement stopped, the governor and his companions attempted to lift the table, yet it would not budge. After conferring with the spirit, the governor was instructed to sit on an adjacent side table. Slowly that table began lifting upward until suspended six inches above the floor with the governor still seated upon it.

Several days later, while in the accompaniment of three ladies, the governor was directed by is spirit friend to retrieve three bells and a guitar from a nearby closet. When those gathered jointly placed their hands upon the table, a bell began to ring. As the melodious and rhythmical chimes subsided, the guitar started its own chorus of soft and gentle strumming. The tones grew louder and bolder before eventually tapering to long vibrating sounds similar to those of distant echoes.

A local medium, Madam Louise, conducted ceremonies dressed in a hooded white séance robe. One of her main spiritual contacts was that of Chief Blackhawk. Born in 1869, Madam Louise grew up in a family well known for their ability to communicate with the deceased. As a prominent doctor and clairvoyant, her father was lauded for his healing skills. Following in her father's footsteps, Louise helped foster a growing trend that created the foundation for the nearby Institute of Spiritualism, an educational facility that its neighbors referred to as the Spook Temple.

Perhaps the area's most established medium was Archibald the Hermit. During the late 1800s, he suddenly estranged himself from his law practice, newspaper business, and society. He proclaimed a vow of poverty and commenced communing with spirits in the town's cemetery. He continued to do so until he suddenly disappeared from the area at the age of seventy-eight.

Though before my time, these characters and the spirits associated with them were destined to connect with me. It never has been easy, and almost impossible, for me to avoid the homegrown ghost. Its main haunts lurk along the old Military Ridge Road. This storied roadway began as a bison trail that became a Native American footpath. It was converted to a regimental route and served as a stagecoach corridor. Later transformed into a major highway, it now is bypassed by a fast-paced interstate. During the years that this course connected Fort Winnebago and Fort Crawford, it was temporarily built as a plank and corduroy road. Due to ruts and rotting timbers, this construction technique never quite succeeded.

Adjacent to the midsection of Military Ridge Road, and just beyond it, are the farms of my sister Kathy, Grandpa Tom, great Grandpa Pete, Uncles Homer and Art, great uncles Ole and Charlie, and great Aunt Christina. Known as the Hollyhead region, much of the surrounding acreage belonged to my Norwegian kin. As such, dealing with the homeland ghost endures as an ongoing family affair.

As a winding thoroughfare, Military Ridge Road stretched through burgs named Frogtown, Minersville, and Patch Diggings. Along the way, the road also shuttled area miners to a jumble of gambling joints called Pokertown. Search diligently and you may find the enduring one-horse settlements of Hyde, Clyde, and Pleasant Ridge. Over the years, most of the once-bustling ore mining hubs have changed names, merged, or just plain disappeared. However, the ghost remains. I can attest to that.

Perhaps it is the ancestry of this rural setting that lends itself to ghostly enclaves. The region's earliest settlers were known as the Effigy Mound Builders who left behind thousands of mysterious burial plots containing bones, pottery, and other artifacts. As Cornish, Welsh, and Irish immigrants moved in to mine the lead and zinc, they were dubbed Badgers because of the dugout hillside burrows that became their homes. Many turned to farming after the depletion of the mineral deposits. Before the burrows were filled in and capped, my father and other kids from his generation used these abandoned tunnels for secret explorations beneath their neighborhoods. At times, the ground has given way as heavy construction equipment treaded across these hidden and hollowed out areas.

Many reminders of this former era still remain. Not far down the road from these old mines is a restored shot tower. Perched on a Cambrian sandstone cliff, it consists of a 120-foot shaft cut through the rock and a 90-foot access tunnel leading to the finishing house. Molten lead poured into a perforated ladle dropped 180 feet and formed shot as it fell to the cooling pool below. The lead shot was loaded onto river barges that were harbored near a location that today serves as a not-so-secret nudist beach. This area was based in Union territory; the lead shot from this tower helped to arm the American Civil War and westward expansion. In its heydays of the mid-1800s, the shot tower operations were frequently visited by a character known as the Scotch Giant, an enormous teamster who drove his ox cart to and from this location.

Surrounding the lead ore smelter was a settlement named Helena that once contended to become the territorial capital. After being snubbed as a railroad passageway, the community dwindled into just another ghost town. Across the river from Helena, an enterprising gal named Iron Lena built one of the area's first houses of pleasure. Known as the Ladies from Hades, this hospitality operation lasted until the lead ran out. It then moved on to the northern logging camps.

Not far from this river valley, there is a region of deep ravines where the locals annually celebrate Ghoulees in the Coulees. Dressed and living like a nineteenth century Native American, the Hiding Kickapoo has often been seen in this area's shadowy backwoods. Wild boars with ghastly tusks harass the farmers around here. Spirits always run amuck in these peculiar places. According to many a legend, they apparently abide in the nearby river as well.

This implicated river is by no means an ordinary waterway. While dissecting the state, it flows for more than 430 miles before emptying into an even larger river. As an example of the eccentricities of this nautical highway, just last year a man paddled half its' length in a hollowed out giant pumpkin. That's nothing compared to River Rat Fred who reputedly lived for years in a floating house dislodged by this river's flood waters. Gronded from time to time on sandbars and along embankments, the navigating residence changed locations whenever a seasonal downpour occurred.

Although appearing docile, beneath this waterway's surface are deadly undercurrents and whirlpools. Well known by area residents, these hazards often create shifting sandbars that are undercut by the river currents. Signs posted alongside its banks forewarn of the dangers.

At one time, I dismissed these devilish legends as nothing more than local folklore. That dismally changed one day during a fishing trip with my buddy Reuben. While sitting on the river bank that faced a sprawling sandbar on the other side, a group of college students decided to make this sandy stretch their afternoon playground. Ignoring the huge parking lot warning sign, one gal naively strolled to the edge of the sandbar. In just a matter of seconds, the footing below her gave way and she vanished. Swallowed by the undertow, she never resurfaced. As Reuben and I watched in horror from across the river, we could hear the screams and cries of her friends. Before long, the rescue boat of the Sheriff's Department arrived, yet it now sadly served as a recovery operation. This destiny has been repeated by those who disrespect these ominous waters.

During the logging era, the river served as an industrial highway. Its upper reaches still conceal age-old logjams where the bones of north woods lumberjacks, known as Pinery boys, remain entangled and trapped. These underwater graveyards are often the cause of disturbances cascading within and below them. Careless boaters, who failed to steer clear of these saturated tombstones, often become added members of the immersed memorials.

After dusk, this river takes on a spooky ambiance as bats and other critters invade the darkness. The crusty fishermen, who angle these unsettling waters for catfish on moonlit nights, often relate tales of morbid shrieks. Some attribute these to the sunken spirits struggling to resurface. Perhaps these sounds are nothing more than screech owls crying in the dark or coyotes prowling the back sloughs. Others hinted that such echoes are emitted by victims of the massasauga swamp rattler. Despite its reclusive nature, it represents an all-too venomous encounter. And indeed, though now few in number, they continue to slither about.

No questions exist as to the reality of the mysterious river whirlpools that old timers called witching waters. However, there was an era when daredevils from a nearby private school defied these anomalies. Resembling a yesteryear extreme sport, they propelled off bridges and dived into the swirling waters. By holding their breath and surrendering to the currents, they rode these whirlpools until literally spit out down river. Although a lofty challenge, this was by no means a risk-free endeavor that the locals considered just plain crazy.

In the highlands above this river valley is the patriarchal farm of my sister. Her pioneer farmhouse dates back to a time just before statehood. Abraham Lincoln is reputed to have rested at this residence while campaigning in 1858 along Military Ridge Road. In those days, there were few places to serve as stopovers, and thus, even a humble farmhouse could become a presidential setting. The locale of this old homestead is not its original site however. It was first built at a crossroads called Four Corners. In the era following its construction, a cholera plague swept through the region. To thwart this scourge, some homes were completely abandoned and others literally moved to isolated locations.

Next to my sister's farm lies Grandpa Tom's place. Hilly and wrinkled with gullies, you would be hard-pressed to find a flat acre on grandpa's land. The farmhouse built on this property was purchased from a 1914 Sears catalog, shipped by rail, and pieced together. The farm evolved into a countryside campus with a three-level barn, milk parlor, machine shed, granary, brooder house, chicken coop, pig pens, cow yard, corn crib, blue Harvester silo, windmill, and two gardens. Also of note is the huge cow yard water trough into which my Uncle Art one day snuck a live two-foot long carp. Grandpa Tom was far from amused by this stunt.

Before my time, there was a fieldstone silo that eventually deteriorated. However, the archaic outhouse still remained and as such, I was bestowed the distinguished honor of tearing it down. While doing so, a rusty nail from the privy punctured my right foot. In the era of cod liver oil and blue bottle elixirs, my prudent grandmother treated my pierced appendage with a standard dousing of blood-red mercurochrome.

At other times, Grandma SeCelia remedied cuts, burns, and abrasions with udder balm. Listerine represented her answer to stinging nettles. A mixture of milk and baking powder was applied to bee or hornet stings. Grandma devised a cure for just about everything, even bouts with the neighbor's dog. After this mutt had repeatedly harassed grandma's chickens, she stormed out of her house, grabbed the dog by the tail, and plastered its behind with turpentine. Dragging its rear end and wailing in retreat, the dog returned never again. One evening, the boys of another neighbor were discovered in the henhouse. They were lucky that they were caught by Grandpa Tom rather than Grandma SeCelia.

Although my lefsa-baking grandma could hold her own against almost anything or anyone, it was Grandpa Tom who pretended to be rough, tough, and gruff. At the end of the day, however, all this dissipated as he pulled out his harmonica, piped out his version of "Redwing," and followed up with an intriguing tale. According to the rural grapevine, he could really cut a rug at barn dances. Nonetheless, throughout more than ninety stubborn years of blood, sweat, and tears, he cleared many a hardscrabble acre and built the family farm.

From my grandfather's farm, I could peer down into a valley where an obscure canyon had been carved out during prehistoric times. Accented by high rock walls, several caves, and a thick tangle of woods, this reclusive chasm was the perfect hideout for characters and creatures unknown. Such seclusion would aptly serve as a haven for native Hodags, even though these rarely seen creatures usually range much farther north. Due to a thick canopy of oaks and maples along its rim, this refuge was often shrouded in perpetual shadows. It was nothing more and nothing less than a haunted hollow.

Just east of Grandpa Tom's place is the abandoned homestead of great Aunt Christina, one of my more storied blood relatives because of her antics in an adjacent state. She and husband Charlie reclaimed great Grandpa Pete's original lodging. A dirt path through the farm fields led to this settlement. My only acquaintance with the immigrant farmhouse was that of a weathered and lifeless place that had been converted over time to a hay storage building. Through its windows, some of which were broken, I could see the hay bales stacked and packed within. It denoted a sparing yet somber fate for my ancestral abode. The nearby tilting barn awaited one more pummeling storm before its collapse. Its rusting windmill and deep well no longer served as a lifeline. After roaming the bordering woods in the darkness, coon hunters often related strange tales about silhouettes and flickering lights in the farmhouse windows. Other accounts muttered about the windmill spinning wildly on windless nights. I still recall quizzing my grandfather as to what he knew of these tales and any local ghosts. Being a master storyteller, Grandpa Tom was never short of words or recollections. In this case, however, his only response was a simultaneous head shake, gruff exhale, and shoulder shrug. This body language indicated that the discussion had ended. As such, I refrained from asking him about the long-ago murder at the nearby Messersmith cheese factory, which many purported as the origin of the area's span of spirit sightings.

Midway between Kathy's and Grandpa Tom's farms rested a dairy land version of the elephant's graveyard. Everything discarded from years of wear and tear lay rusting in this intriguing treasury. Two broken down farm trucks, an elderly John Deere tractor, antiquated horse-drawn machinery, a hay wagon loaded with worn out tools and iron parts were easily spotted. Busted barrels, piles of coffee cans and canning jars, blue medicine bottles, syrup jugs, dented milk cans, crushed water troughs, rotted fence posts, coils of vintage barbed wire, and a cache of weather-bleached cow bones also shared this pastoral dump site. Weird sounds often echoed as the wind rustled through this decaying collection. As a memorial to hard times and hard labor, this was a place for reverence rather than recycling. Even more so, it represented the perfect hideout for rattlesnakes, woodchucks, and the occasional ghost.

Just a short distance from this "junkdom," there is a second depository piled at the bottom of a bluff. This is where my dad aided Uncle Art in pushing his beyond-repair Star car over a rocky outcropping and watched it nosedive into decades of tumbled trash. With no use or place for a beat-up jalopy, this was by no means an unusual event. Prior to the emergence of salvage yards, scrapped vehicles were haphazardly discarded in this manner. Local hunters can attest that many bluff bottoms exhibit the rusted remains of bygone machines and metal parts. Perhaps they might even dare to whisper about a fabled presence near these skeletal sites.

Dating back to the horse and buggy days, tales of the Military Ridge ghost have spirited about for a century and more. Over the decades, speculation on this homegrown specter has resulted in varied spine-tingling accounts. Traveling salesmen and doctors on house calls often spoke of being followed by eerie green lights. Some surmise that the earliest sightings began after a young man was killed in a tavern brawl near Pottsville. Others refer to the Messersmith murder.

Perhaps the most chilling rendition relates to the pastor of Saint Bridget's Church. While descending the parsonage stairway, this parish priest suspiciously tripped and ended up dead at the bottom threshold. Following this tragedy, witnesses claimed that blood seeped through the wainscoting woodwork each day at the same staircase spot and at 3:00 PM—the time of his demise. As a macabre coincidence, lightening struck the church and burned it to the ground in a short time. Abandoning the remaining parish manor in its rural setting, the congregation built a new Saint Bridget's Church in a nearby town. Eventually, the stranded rectory withered from decay and desolation. What remained was the everlasting question of whether this priest had been attacked by the ghost or indeed had become a ghost himself.

Another ill-fated soul is alleged to have died not from an encounter with the ghost but due to his exodus. During an early evening work departure, a local meat cutter named Lewis was midway home on the rural road to his house. Looking ahead, he saw what appeared to be an approaching green light. As he moved closer to the light, it showcased a rampaging carriage without a driver or passengers. Standing silently and staring, Lewis became awestruck as the carriage glowed brighter and levitated skyward above him. He then dashed all the way home, stumbled onto the porch, and never stood again. Put to bed in an extremely weakened condition, Lewis died the next day with his once fully dark hair as white as snow.

Unlike Grandpa Tom, my sister does not hesitate to elaborate on the ghostly encounters within her home. Many are the times when Kathy awakes to find objects rearranged throughout her house. Now and then, dormant clocks, silent radios, and electrical items suddenly come to life on their own. Although this seems more mischievous than malicious, there are compelling events that oblige an explanation of this dwelling. According to my sister, these paranormal escapades are simply the ramblings of her husband's great grandmother, who hung herself in this residence to escape the writhing pain of a terminal illness. Her lingering presence continues to align and array this house to her own liking. Even their dog's behavior seems affected by this haunting presence.

On one occasion, Kathy and my daughter Brianna witnessed the semblance of a shadowy cloaked figure that tarried in the nearby pasture before disappearing. At other times, images of wooly black dogs and dark shaggy horses have sauntered through the surrounding acres. The horse manifestation is often linked to Argelius, the nineteenth century horse thief. Not long ago, a red kangaroo was captured after hopping about in frost-covered hayfields near Kathy's farm. Where it came from and how it got here, no one knows. However, conjecture pointed to ties between this critter from down under and the resident ghost.

Although most things unexplained in this region are usually blamed on the infamous phantom, I often viewed these events with a fair amount of skepticism. All this changed one day in a matter of minutes. On a late October afternoon, my wife Dianna and I embarked to gather cornstalks to bundle as a corn shock decoration. After stopping at Kathy's farm, we were surprised to find no one about. We then ventured off to Grandpa Tom's farm and again encountered the same chilling sense of abandonment. No life seemed to stir at either farm. It felt unsettling to be the only ones milling about.

Nonetheless, the two of us set off to complete our mission. Walking down the hillside toward the nearest cornfield, we were greeted by harvested acreage where nothing but stubble remained. Looking around us, the neighboring cornfields had also been husked away for grain and silage. Wandering through the empty fields, I was reminded of the story told to me by my Uncle Homer. One morning while preparing to milk the cows, Homer's chores were interrupted by a clamor south of the barn. Stepping outside, he immediately observed that dozens of Canadian geese had invaded the cornfield. Grabbing the 12-guage stored in the barn, Homer ventured toward the feathered crooks. Startled by his presence, the entire flock erupted upward into the autumn dawn. In a reflex response, Homer shouldered the shotgun and pulled back on the trigger. To his surprise, six geese dropped from the sky. This incredible single-shot fete resulted in an ample supply of down for Grandma Se Celie's pillows.

Disappointed by not gathering any stalks for a seasonal corn shock, Dianna and I headed back to my grandfather's house. Just as we stepped onto the walkway leading to his residence, Dianna pointed to a strange object whirling in the sky above the old dumpsite. Still at a fair distance away, the object appeared to be moving toward us. It hovered hundreds of feet in the air and spun wildly like a rotating helicopter blade. For whatever reason, this celestial curiosity continued on a straight course until positioned directly above us. Without warning, this spinning specter rapidly descended from the heavens and landed at our feet. To our amazement, what now lay before us was nothing more than a cornstalk. Fortunately, I quickly realized the symbolic revelation. This was an omen, a message, a demonstration of sorts, and definitely a case for "seeing is believing". We dared not try to explain or challenge the conundrum. Instead, our immediate and fleeting departure left us sensing without a doubt, we had just been stalked by a ghost. Needless to say, we indubitably ended up with a corn shock.

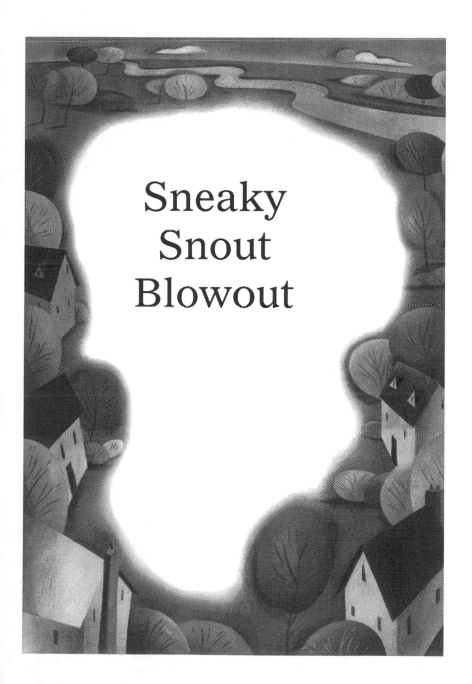

Sneaky
Snout
Blowout

Once upon a town untangled, just north of here, a freak of nature was held captive in a chicken-wire enclave. To many, it was one of the ugliest creatures they had ever seen. The bulbous body and snouted face of this critter repulsed all who gazed upon it. Even more hideous was the white scruffy beard dangling beneath its chin and often drool-drenched from slobbering jowls. Only extreme pity would make anyone feel the slightest affection toward this brute. Perhaps that is why my brother threw caution to the wind on this fateful day when he fool heartedly approached it for a close encounter of the worst kind.

This story begins with two places of similar names. Both are longtime farmers' markets with family labels. One is called Heck's and the other Peck's. To those not akin to this area, this always causes confusion on the east to west drive along Highway 14. First comes Heck's, then there is Peck's. Still further down the road is Peck's again. Remembering which is which creates anxiety for some. Not so for the wise and wary who know that Heck's represents the vast lawn ornament ensemble and perennial weekend flea market. Peck's showcases a petting zoo, giant jack-o'-lantern, horse-drawn hay wagons, and an occasional camel ride. The petting zoo is a tourist trap for animal lovers. It is a menagerie of miniature goats, peacocks, prairie dogs, wallabies, pheasants, albino deer, buffalo, burros, and other critters. There is also a trout pool, goose pond, and alligator den. It attracts locals and visitors from afar.

The markets are overloaded with fresh produce, squeaky cheese curds, Amish cashew brittle, cinnamon bread, giant freakish squash, goofy gourds, seasonal flowers, and other country delights. It is almost impossible to drive by without stopping at one market or the other. Peck's however, had an enticing edge in family appeal with its deceiving façade that fiendishly masked the dangers within. So it was that my brother Scott and his family were lured to this place on an unsuspecting midsummer day for nothing more than an innocent petting zoo visit. To get there, they travelled north of town on the same route often ventured by the Scotch Giant, Iron Lena, and Blackhawk. This also meant cruising past the conspicuous barn with a Boeing 377 Stratofreighter parked alongside it and then passing the enchanted house embedded in a bluff, where behemoth sea monsters, carnival carousels and strange anomalies reside. Farther down the road stands that hillside castle called Taliesen. A field of abandoned stump trolls appears next. Finally after crossing over the river of witching waters and turning east, the destination is reached.

Sometimes, making an impression requires going above and beyond the normal scheme of things. Such was the case when my brother decided to entertain his three-year-old daughter Alyssa by pretending to pucker up and kiss the pot-bellied pig. I had been to this petting zoo and knew of this semi-sweet swine. Far from being a rip-snorting Razorback or psychotic squealer with a squeamish personality, he was a friendly chap with the typical pudgy profile. Of course, this included a billowing ground-dragging belly. Descending beneath the grunter's chin was a white scruffy beard, drenched in drool and dangling under slobbering jowls. From his flat-fronted nozzle to midway below both ears, the mouth of this portly fellow curved upward into an impish sneer. A curlicue tail spiraled over his chubby backside cheeks. Upholstered in a rough bristle-hair hide with mud accents, the term cuddly did not apply to such beasts. Like all pot-bellied pigs, however, this porker was so homely that you considered it cute in a most pitiful manner.

Being congenial, the diminutive piggy never hesitated to greet people by jumping against the wire fence. Balancing on his hind legs, the hog leaned forward to gaze into the visitor's eyes. He exhibited zoo pandering at its best. As an attempt to make this an eventful outing, my brother's plan included walking directly to the pig, bending over for a face-to-face encounter, and pretending to kiss the consenting critter. Everything went according to plan, almost. With his anxious daughter watching in anticipation, dad stooped forward to express his amorous affections. In doing so, the pig immediately responded by lunging up onto the fence railing, hunched forward, and without any warning, sneezed. The unpredicted full-gale dousing was punctuated with heavy precipitation or what some might call a tsunami of snot. As no mere sniffle and a gust unworthy of a *gesundheit*, this nasal assault lathered Scott's face with a boorish barrage, literally pork roasting him for hamming it up. At first, Alyssa stood spellbound momentarily and then screamed. Meanwhile, while becoming hysterical with laughter, his wife Darci accidently stepped backward and slipped into a huge mud puddle.

At the sight of all this, Alyssa was unsure whether to cry or laugh. Taking a cue from the smirking pig, she opted for the later and begged her dad to do it again. Dad, however, had already pigged out on more than enough of the sweet and sour pork. Never, never, never again, would he allow himself to go hog wild and pucker up to a pot-bellied porky—not by the hairs of any pig's chinny-chin-chin. For now, the only remedy was to head home and grill some pork chops, complete with side orders of ribs and ham. Perhaps some chitlin's and pickled pigs' feet could be added as well. No need to turn kosher or be hamstrung after such hogwash.

When it comes to piggish pursuits, Scott was not the only family member to hog all the attention. During visits to Grandpa Tom's farm, my brother Tom and I took it upon ourselves to harass the hogs. Whenever we were bored with swinging like Tarzan in the hayloft and knew that gramps was out in the fields, it became time for a pigpen roundup. Fenced within an area half the size of a football field, our stern Norwegian grandfather maintained an enclosure for yearling oinkers and a separate shelter of motherly sows. As an act of barnyard bedlam, my brother and I would climb in to this pen from opposite sides. The whole idea was to see which one of us could rile these pigs into a frenzied stampede toward the other. During one of these escapades, I found a rope and decided to lasso a lard belly. Unable to succeed, I turned to ingenuity and laid the looped end on the ground. With Tom's assistance, the pigs were driven toward this foot snare. As the first porker stepped into the loop, I yanked back quickly and found that my scheme had worked. Tugging and snorting like a wild boar, the strength of my captive had been grossly underestimated. Caught off balance, I found myself stumbling into the less than pleasant pigsty. Still holding on to the rope and scrambling to my feet, it dawned on me that I now needed to get close enough to untwine the hog tied swine.

Due to good fortune, some desperate prayers, and mostly poor knot-tying skills, the rope and pig suddenly parted ways. Just in the nick of time, Tom and I were saved. Had the knot remained raveled, Grandpa Tom would have surely unraveled upon witnessing our pig rustling. Thank God in hog heaven that none of the pigs squealed on us. Taking this reprieve into consideration, we abandoned any future plans of trying to ride these critters.

During my college dating days, I decided to impress my future wife Dianna with a tour of the rustic countryside around my hometown. Upon turning down the gravel road alongside Cutlure Creek, our hearts and the car came to an abrupt stop. From a brushy area lining this road, an enormous sow suddenly jumped out to block our progress. Dianna began screaming in terror as her big city background had not prepared her for such an encounter. She kept hollering, "What is that pig doing here and why is it staring at me?" You would have thought we were on an African safari with an irritable rhino challenging us. Runaway bacon is not a routine sight in this neck of the woods, so I really had no answer to Dianna's panic. However, in what seemed like déjà vu, I sensed previous ties to this porker and noticed what appeared to be a rope-burn scar on its hind leg. Nonetheless, in a disparaging snort of discontent, the horrendous beast departed, and so did we.

As an urbanite, Dianna deserves credit for properly identifying this barnyard behemoth. That was not the case, however, involving one peculiar out-of-state hunter. This metropolitan marksman drove around town while showing off his first deer kill. He finally was stopped by local authorities who needed to know why a hog was tied atop his vehicle. And some wonder why the local yokels are so pigheaded about not allowing outsiders to hunt in these parts. However, there is now a county just north of here where feral pigs run wild and no one minds if a frequent potshot is aimed their way.

Despite the pigmented perils, none of the outcomes from these pig tales has harbored any hard feelings. In fact, all of this baloney has me craving for a pizza loaded with sausage and bacon. Might as well go high on the hog and order an extra large. Hopefully, this won't result in making a pig of myself.

The Reunion

O nce upon a town untangled, there flowed a magical stream of murky waters and secret places. Alongside it, a narrow path had been etched by the footprints of an old master and his apprentice. They sought out and battled the scaly monsters residing within the depths of these waters. Many times they had to elude the shrieking sentries who guarded this lair and readily plucked out the eyes of intruders. The snorting beast that grazed in the pasture nearby had to be accounted for as well. Though this duo did not always prevail in their streamside pursuits, nonetheless, they never returned without an embellished tale to tell. Then came that day when the stories ended and a reunion endlessly beckoned.

No reunion ever occurs without risk. You take your chances and hope for the best. It is possible that nothing has changed, yet it is more probable that many things have. Perhaps it will be you who is the most notable of any changes. That, in and of itself, can be good or bad. This reunion was never destined to be anything ordinary. It had been in the planning stages for more than two decades and would rekindle an old friendship that somehow became distant as one grew restless and the other grew mossy. Both were inevitable.

Over the years, life began enticing me farther and farther away from my old stomping grounds. Fame and fortune now seemed to be much more important than youthful pursuits such as angling excursions with Reuben, my fishing buddy and the sovereign Master of Mill Creek. When it came to trout fishing, his virtuosity was beyond comparison. I was the protégé to Reuben's mentorship. As angling experts, we both were purists, who purely dunked night crawlers and a few secret baits into the local waterways. More often than not, this meant Mill Creek.

A venture about most rural back roads eventually leads to a meandering stream dubbed Mill Creek. It is one of the more common names because of the numerous old immigrant mills that once dotted the countryside. The Mill Creek I befriended still had its antiquated mill and the giant wooden waterwheel that rotated as currents cascaded over the adjacent damn. Rebuilt in 1850 after a suspicious scorching, the mill continued as a sawmill and later was converted to a grist grinder. Below this elderly laborer, a deep and foaming pool quickly narrowed into a slow-moving tributary. Bordered by cow pastures and cultivated fields, a muddy runoff forever mingled in these waters. After a heavy rainfall, it resembled a ribbon of chocolate milk pouring through dairy land. Although this never created the image of a crystal clear and pristine fishery, those who knew how to fish Mill Creek usually came home with a creel full of trout and fishy tales.

Above the dam, Mill Creek's waters were a little less tinted, faster moving, and shallow. Below it, everything became deeper, murkier, and more sluggish. In the upper reaches, the trout were plentiful, but smaller. The lower section seemed reserved for the lonesome lunkers. Under Reuben's tutelage, I was well mentored on catching both. Because this stream eventually emptied into a major river, there were often surprises at the end of the line such as big ol' catfish, northern pike, bullheads, bluegills, bass, and despicable carp. Still, it was trout that ruled this stream, and Reuben who reigned over the trout.

Although Reuben owned and drove two different cars, his 1949 Chevy coupe served as the official fishing clunker. This motorized tackle box had a backseat and trunk crammed with all sorts of gear. After so many years of successful outings, it took on an angling aroma of fish scales and leftover bait. True enthusiasts would never take offense to such sensual surroundings, yet Reuben's wife refused to set foot in this car. Like Reuben, it was weathered, aging, and always ready for the next streamside safari. Stomping down on the clutch and shifting away, Reuben and his six-banger never failed to complete a hook, line, and sinker mission.

Reuben was a widower who married a gal named Olive, who also had lost her spouse. In his signature polka dot hat and witty stories, Reuben drew lots of attention. Olive's unique character commanded much the same. Somewhat on the heavy side and tremendously bow-legged, she often roamed her yard with an obsession to destroy every dandelion. Each time she bent over and her dress rose higher, my mom Esther lamented about acquiring a slingshot and just once firing away at the all too tempting target. Nowadays, crafters market lawn signs to remind us of such bloomer clad butts. Hard-laboring Olive was the original however.

No one knew the Mill Creek area better than Reuben. As a CCC {AU: Explain what this is please.}boy during the Depression era, he worked on many of the roads that led to the trout stream. Reuben had been fishing Mill Creek even before its headwaters spillway was built. His footprints had touched every embankment alongside this waterway.

During early spring excursions, Reuben and I routinely contended with a familiar nemesis. Mill Creek was a spawning ground for hordes of disgusting suckers. The term rough or trash fish aptly applied to these dimwit denizens. Aside from a dogfish or sheepshead, there really is nothing uglier then these freshwater freaks. Unlike the prominent hooked jaw of a salmon or toothy grin of a muskie, suckers were bestowed with mud-sucking nozzles. Their designer must have concentrated on function and abandoned all style in this design. Even when hooked, these bait-stealers would simply roll on the surface without even putting up a decent fight.

On my first river outing with Reuben, I hooked a huge redhorse, a scalier version of a sucker with bright red fins and tails. The same day, my catch also included a mudpuppy, which I didn't know even existed in this river. The following weekend, we landed a garfish and shovel-nosed sturgeon. Later on, we shared the experience of unhooking sheepsheads as they grossly belched in protest. Occasionally, bewhiskered mud cats and bullheads would interrupt our day. My one and only encounter with a dogfish was like staring into the face of a prehistoric predator. Thanks to Reuben, I confronted far too many of the underwater uglies. The seasonal opening for trout fishing always served as a welcome respite from this riverbed of weirdos. However, even the best of trout havens were often shared by the bottom feeders.

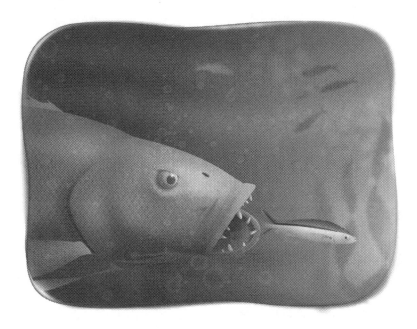

If you are what you eat, I fail to understand how anyone could consume a mud forager. Reuben, however, had a friend who smoked suckers. Therefore, we often kept a stringer full of suckers during spring runs. That experience ended for me one day when I encountered my first Stephen King moment. While fishing one of our favorite trout holes, a deep pool created by a tumbled oak across the stream, Reuben and I had hooked half a dozen suckers. We secured them on a chain stringer that was tied to the fallen tree and extended into the water. This was a memorable fishing hole where each of us had hooked and lost the brown trout of our dreams. Reuben claimed this behemoth trout had spots on it the size of quarters. Neither of us knew what to expect when fishing this haven.

Such was the case on this ill-fated day when we prepared to head home and pulled up our stringer of suckers. As I did so, my entire being became unsettled. Dangling from the metal stringer was a cryptic collection of six disembodied fish. Staring back at me were the bugged eyes of the remaining nozzle-nosed heads. What deepwater demon had executed such abomination? Was it the giant trout, a snapping turtle, an otter, or perhaps something not of this world? For a long time, I stayed clear of this peculiar place, not wanting any further exchanges with whatever skulked within this vile underwater lair.

Beyond the banks of this waterway, other dangers awaited as well. As the chorus of red-winged blackbirds echoed across the nearby meadows and marshes, their songs were more than just melodies. These were the war cries of nesting ninjas. Should any of these feathered demons be residing nearby, it was wise to avoid this stretch of stream. An encounter with sharp beaks scraping across exposed scalps or the gouging out of eyeballs was of valid concern. So too were the sinister snorts of a galloping ghost that roamed this valley and stood sentry over grazing dairy cows.

Though bulls were kept out of the pastures, one particular herd of Holsteins had a guardian of its own. It was a horse possessed—an unbridled pastoral poltergeist. If our bank side wanderings led us anywhere near these cows, this devilish equine would storm hell-bent from its hidden post with nostrils flaring and hoofs flailing. Twice I found myself dashing for the nearest fence line to escape the beast. Unlike the fabled Scottish Kelpie pony that entices its victims into the water before thrashing them into demise, this steed just wanted to scare the bajeebers out of us. We never could be quite sure where the hooligan lurked as the cattle grazed up and down the valley. Although none of the local farmers ever claimed ownership to this bad news bronc, its exchanges in the valley below Military Ridge were far from friendly.

Despite its associated hazards, fishing Mill Creek was always worth the effort. Somehow, over the years, other priorities in my life enticed me away from this cherished trout stream. My fishing soul however, never let go of Mill Creek memories and its prospects. I desperately needed a reunion, yet I always allowed for excuses that kept me away. Finally, when the opportunity came to move back to this area, the reunion became inevitable. I coerced my youngest brother Scott to join me in meeting an old friend. Familiar with my endless tales of fishing fantasies, he readily agreed. Fully equipped with enthusiasm and expertise, we headed for the countryside. Along the way, I kept thinking about Reuben, whose spirit still flowed, even though his life had ended far too early because of cancer. As such, I would now be the mentor to a younger apprentice. These were enormous shoes to fill.

Lacking the angling attire and aroma, my brother's vehicle paled in comparison to the character of Reuben's trout mobile. Rolling along on blacktop that I recalled as gravel roads, it did not take long to notice the changes. Many farm fields had transformed into the landscaped lawns of upscale homesteads. The remaining fields were cultivated to the very edge of stream boundaries. As a result, trees that had shaded Mill Creek and fortified bank sides had been purged. Wetlands doubling as pastures now were converted to cornfields. The once sturdy fence lines lay fallen from years of neglect. The remaining upright fence posts that refused to buckle held signs shouting "No Trespassing." In the midst of it all, a fickle creek twisted in all directions.

Further downstream, an antique mill with its idle waterwheel and adjacent gift shop greeted visitors as a tourist attraction. A prominent sign noting the history of the site stood nearby. A companion sign quoted a long judicial review of the fishing governance currently bestowed on this waterway. The worm dunkers that Reuben and I proudly represented were no longer welcome. Everything from hook styles to bait choice was under regulatory siege. For the sake of preservation, politics replaced what had been a prized pastime. This reunion, however, was not over yet. Perhaps there would be downstream stretches offering greater hospitality.

Although it was Reuben who first brought me to Mill Creek, I now had to reacquaint myself without his introductions. As clouds rolled in and a storm threatened, I began advising my brother as how we would quickly proceed downstream and test our luck at several favorite spots. A familiar bend in the creek served as an omen. A deep pool that had once languished here was sadly shallow. The cascading rapids below it lulled to nothing more than a trickle. The only solution was to continue downstream to where the undercut banks had sheltered some of my biggest catches. However, each bend in the stream brought the same results. The depths had descended amidst subtle currents. Gone were the undercuts that served as hideouts and the water-cooling tree canopies. A disgusting pile of beer cans left behind by some oaf triggered the thought that a stiff drink was truly needed at this moment.

Without further surveillance, it was now time to retreat from this reunion. In the process of doing so, I sensed something unfamiliar. No other fishermen had been spotted on this day. Gone were the grazing cows and their need for a ghoulish guardian. Gone as well were any signs of the wood ducks and otters that once resided here. An eerie absence of war cries from the red-winged warriors spooked me even more so. These now depleted waters could barely harbor any deepwater demons. At one time, certain sections of this stream were more than six-feet deep. Reuben had proved that during one outing.

Some sort of exorcism had rid this domain of all spirits, both good and evil. Vanished was the magic that once gilded Mill Creek. I wondered how Reuben would have viewed this calamity. However, the fishing buddy who once drove a six-cylinder tackle box, who taught me how to carve green willow whistles, and who always had a tale to tell when the fish weren't biting, no longer sat beside me on these muddy banks. Perhaps this was the real reason the magic had faded. It was not the reunion I had anticipated nor longed for. My empty creel lacked both fins and dreams. Still, all was not lost as I hooked and landed memories of a master and mentor. Regardless of the flow, they never run dry. And the lesson learned here is that there are no regulations or bag limits on fish stories.

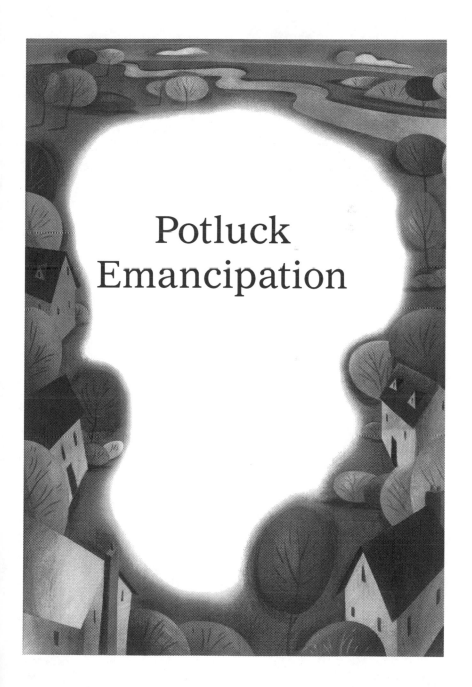

Potluck
Emancipation

Once upon a town untangled, the law of the land decreed that men rule and women obey. It was a sobering reality in those times. Soon, however, all this would change due to an intoxicating turn of events made possible by a humble stump grubber, his widowed mother, and a high-strung tradition shot down in its prime.

Although this story is about booze and bodacious women, it also involves a civil rights showdown; one that was bitterly triggered at the end of a rope. Near an old secluded homestead, just three miles from town, a group of armed farmers and their kin gathered together. What started out as a peaceful encounter suddenly went haywire as two lethal shots rang out. Next came a staggering frenzy that was anything but sedate. At the heart of all this, stood a stump grubber named Jack and a ballistic widow gone wild.

When it came to stump grubbing, Jack was among the best. Area farmers were well acquainted with his notorious skills for clearing the land. Few had Jack's drive and determination for stump grubbing. This rigorous task required a muscular man to spend hours, if not days, hacking away at age old roots in order to remove trees, one by one, from a farmer's acreage. Although chains and sturdy draft horses were frequently part of this endeavor, it mostly took calloused hands and a huge pick axe to complete the chore. Oftentimes, it also required a crock of healing hooch to ease the pain associated with a long day's labor. Local gossip attested to Jack seeking this treatment quite often.

In the wooded hollow east of Grandpa Tom's farm and just up the hill from the Mill Creek spillway, Jack resided with his mother in a rustic family cabin. It was a paltry and independent lifestyle, well suited to both of them. Jack was a perennial bachelor and not likely to change his status. Being a reclusive character, he lived off the land whenever stump grubbing demands were idle. Jack had the renowned reputation of a cagey hunter who could track down and consume just about any critter that roamed the woodlands. Uncle Homer was a nearby neighbor. He stopped by one day at noontime to visit Jack and was immediately invited in for lunch. Upon entering the kitchen, Jack propped open the oven door and proudly displayed a roasting whistle pig, or what most refer to as a woodchuck. The sight of this skinned varmint with all four legs sticking straight up swayed my uncle from making any additional mealtime visits.

Although Jack would never have been labeled a ladies' man, it can be said that he certainly impacted the lives of many local womenfolk. Without a doubt, both Jack and his mother should be credited as homespun pioneers of emancipation. In this neck of the woods, even stump grubbers could sometimes evolve into equal rights activists without knowing it.

Jack was a friendly chap and well liked by those who knew him. As a celebration of this friendship, Jack made it an annual tradition to shed his reclusive nature and invite area farmers to his homestead following the fall harvest. This event involved the men and older boys bringing their guns and joining Jack in a grand safari. As for the women and children, their roles included preparing the baked goods and maintaining a giant boiling cauldron. Upon returning from the hunt, the collective bounty would be skinned and deposited into the steaming cast iron kettle. The luck of this hunt served as an early rendition for what eventually became known as a potluck. With deer not as plentiful like they are nowadays, this potluck normally consisted of squirrels, rabbits, and a grouse or two. If by chance a possum, weasel, fox, or raccoon was found wandering about, these too would be added to the bounty. Fortunately, skunks, badgers, weasels, and woodchucks had usually sought underground hibernation by now. Otherwise, Jack would likely have insisted on adding them as well. What he did with coyotes remains uncertain.

This Thanksgiving event of sorts had another element attached to its tradition. For many of the farmers, the gregarious gathering represented not only a well-earned respite from fieldwork but also an annual opportunity to imbibe while their spouses refrained from the obligatory scrutiny. To truly celebrate, Jack required that a keg of homebrew be brought in to wash down each year's feast. Along with this demand, it was also deemed necessary that the keg be hoisted high into a tree and secured until the hunt concluded. This was a precautionary safeguard to prevent any pilfering of this precious brew while the men were out scouring the fields and forest.

Because of the keg's sheer size and weight, this high-strung tactic worked well to deter any parched women from liberating the elevated ale and sampling its contents. Although the thirst for home brew could never be limited to just masculine taste buds, the rule that the keg remain in its lofty perch was obediently honored by the women. However, it just so happened that during one particular year, Jack's mother had an insatiable quench for something more. Needing to add some folly and perhaps a legacy to her life's story, the time had come for a down home toast to equality.

After the men secured the nesting brew and departed for their hunt, Jack's mother started debating the need for her and the other women to create a happy hour of their own. Although Jack's mother conceded to honoring the treetop keg tradition, she surmised that no rule existed to prevent consumption of its contents during its heightened state. As the women pondered the predicament, Jack's mother arranged to have several wash tubs and copper boilers brought out from her cabin for placement directly below the keg. She then walked back into her home and quickly reappeared with one of Jack's loaded rifles. With an awestruck assembly watching, many holding hands to their faces, Jack's mother ambled over to an area just beyond the keg. Bracing the rifle snugly against her right shoulder and aiming upward, she pulled back on the trigger and fired away. From the holes that now punctured the keg's oak bottom and sides, a foaming stream cascaded outward. Shuffling about, the jubilant onlookers quickly rearranged the copper boilers to collect the fermented waterfall.

It is not really clear how much time expired before the men returned from their hunt. As the riflemen trickled in, they stumbled upon a sight caused by what had trickled out. Before them was an unloaded keg and overloaded women. A long tradition of tee-totaling had been tapped out. To say the least, Jack's annual outing was now witness to a bondage unburdened. The hangover from this savory revolution would soon recover into an endless evolution of changing times.

On a gala autumn day, when a grand feast unfolded, food for thought was served as well. Born in a backwoods setting, the catalyst for change had emerged. Due to Jack's hosting of this potshot festivity and his mother's audacious activism, inebriation liberation spilled out into these times. A mere shot in the right direction nourished the craving for something more. In a tipsy fashion, an insurmountable barrier was barreled over at the modest homestead of a hardworking stump grubber and his madcap mama. In doing so, plundered prohibition now gave birth to potluck emancipation. According to my Grandpa Tom, this entire state of affairs was enough to drive one to drinking.

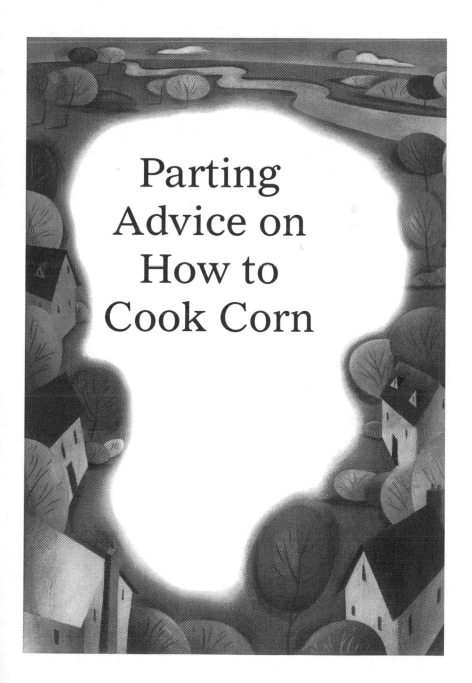

Parting Advice on How to Cook Corn

Once upon a town untangled, a time of reckoning had finally come to herald the unheralded and venerate those whose virtues rarely are recognized. This encompasses drunkards, dumps, demons, duffers, delinquents, and the downtrodden. Additionally included are fishing buddies, featherbrains, family pets, pot bellied pigs, stump grubbers, sharpshooters, spinsters, spirits, and spiritual mentors. Perhaps creepy crawlers, giants, horse thieves, and river rats should also be noted. Together, this cast of characters endures as an all-too-familiar place called hometown.

Regardless of size and nature, each town has a storied past. Whether its residents are hayseeds, yokels, or city slickers is inconsequential. However, upon digging into any town's heritage, be cautious of all items unearthed. Take heed of anything entangled. Oftentimes, there is more than what meets the eye. As such, prepare to sense that which may not always make sense. And know that startling surprises will surely occur.

Even though it may not be possible to go back to what was in the past, certain things just need to be recollected. My beastly mansion is no longer a residence. Not so long ago it was converted to a law office and now serves as a social services agency. The St; Joseph's Church that I once knew has been torn down and replaced by modern architecture. The hospital bears a new moniker with no saintly labeling. Piggly Wiggly relocated and competes with the new WalMart. The Spinster sisters lay buried, yet where is unknown. Mill Creek continues as a trickle of what it use to be. Before despairing that all has changed however, it needs to be noted that drunkards, muskies, and rambunctious juveniles still prowl about. The resident ghost does the same as well.

Within my homegrown bumpkin patch, many of us are sometimes viewed as slightly out of our gourds. That's okay, because it has never been necessary for everyone to ripen the same way or even the same day. Instead, it all comes down to caretaking and cultivation. Next, is the determination of what gets weeded out and what does not. By routinely adding an ample amount of enriching fertilizer, everything continues to grow. Therefore, the secret to hometown legacies is to keep piling it on while reminiscing.

Should you choose to harvest your own stories, make it a bounty of homegrown literary sweet corn, thoroughly buttered and take with a grain of salt. If by chance some of it becomes too sappy, well then, consider this plain ol' corn syrup. Anything quite serious is nothing more than corn starch. As for the most intoxicating testimony, let it go down as soothing corn squeezins' or what some call sour mash. Although these servings may not satisfy all appetites, there is no need to fret as long as everything is done in good taste. Just readily and forever keep in mind when mixing this recipe, there really is no place like home. So be it.

Folklore for Real:
A Primer

Once upon a time soon to come, you will untangle your hometown. First and hence forth, you must become familiar with one's own folklore. Also required will be the separating of facts from fiction. Doing so demands serious sleuthing and a well cultivated grapevine.

According to Webster, folklore is the customs and traditions of a people. Some snobs have the audacity to think that it is nothing more than nonsense and make believe. Nothing could be further from the truth. Because all hometowns have a storied past, to discover the folklore of yours requires extensive research and reliable gossip. Although the later is not often hard to come by, the former can involve many twists and turns. Most folklore has an authentic basis which oftentimes becomes embellished over the years.

To explore the folklore of your community, start with your County and State Historical Societies. Most have both websites and museums. The next step in this quest may appear surprising. You must begin following the postcard trail. When postcards began being produced back in the 1800's, their purpose was that of a documentary rather than tourism enticement. During the advent of photography, the shutterbugs entering this trade, often travelled regionally and prospered by the sales of their pictured accounts. Their wares varied anywhere from a shot of the local railroad depot to that whimsical round barn on the outskirts of town. Street scenes, churches, schools, and courthouses were also favorites. Even area asylums could be found on postcards, although this seems perplexing, as from whom or to whom, such a card would be sent.

Another standard for researching the past is old newspapers and magazines. However, two other printed materials sometimes get overlooked. Vintage school yearbooks often display not only the students and staff, yet showcase long forgotten businesses who served as sponsors. Commemorative books also display storied pasts. These can range from the anniversary of a neighborhood church to the town's centennial. Finally, grade school readers from way back when, contain interesting items that no longer appear in today's textbooks.

Never underestimate the makeup of any community, both past and present. While naming the people, places, and dates, history books overlook far too much of the folklore. Some things to compare and expand upon include:

HALLOWED HAVENS: Even humble places can have their nearby castles. Hereabouts, one is called the House on the Rock and the other Taliesin. Within my hometown is the meager cabin of the first territorial governor. As for the beastly mansion and similar havens, there are many scattered throughout. These antiquated enclaves are the former homes of founding fathers and muckety-mucks. Some are perhaps haunted. That's just the way it is in most hometowns. Mingled among the mansions are bungalows, saltboxes, brownstones, Tudors, colonials, Cape Cods, and a few gingerbread houses, some almost too small to occupy. Several old barns and one room schoolhouses have become residences as well. Not far from here are the Pendarvis homes of Cornish miners. However, one area abode which perplexes me, belongs to the local stonecutter, who chisels the monuments and digs the graves. Next to his business, he built an underground family home. Now give that some deep contemplation.

SACRED PLACES: In looking back, there's a good possibility you will discover that your town's past had a greater diversity of churches than now exists. This was often due to the early influx of immigrants, many preferring their own houses of worship. Down home politics usually dictated just which churches flourished and remained. Some even underwent radical changes, such as the Rock Ridge country church northeast of my hometown. It converted to a hippie commune during the early 70's. According to my sister, the longhairs are still there. As a different sort of transformation, an enterprising businessman decided to salvage the steeple from the main street Methodist church, when it became necessary to demolish this building. Lifted by crane onto a truck, the steeple was then hauled to his country inn, where it now serves as a storybook honeymoon suite. Some country churches have also been transformed into summer cottages and hunting lodges. My favorite conversion however, is a neighboring town church turned gift shop and named "Bats in the Belfry".

QUIRKY CHARACTERS: The folklore of every hometown relies on peculiar personalities.   These are the people who add interest to our lives by just being themselves.   Perhaps one of them represents the town's version of a Keystone cop.   Another might be the reclusive old codger who is a spitting image of Santa.   Then there is that motor-head always showing off his supercharged muscle car.   Not to be overlooked is the unheralded kid who spent his high school days in special ed and now performs every odd job around.   Also, do not ignore that overloaded neighbor with an awful lot on his awful lot.   Possibly, even a pair of mysterious sisters, saunter up and down your main street. Each and everyone, reigns as a part of the local landscape.

Chances are that lubricated locals have become some of the most noticed characters in your town.   Notorious drinking habits date back to the pioneer days when consuming alcohol was considered safer than drinking water.   Booze consumption use to be deemed a cure for ills and a means to enliven the aged.   Though times have changed, habits have not.   Every hometown grapevine can attest to this.   Both comic and tragic, staggering citizenries are sobering realities.   Around here, if you wish to see the more amusing side of inebriation, just attend a wedding reception and watch tipsy relatives trying to chicken dance or hokey pokey.

DOWNHOME HAPPENINGS: Everyone needs a routine cure for monotony.   No matter how modest the event, even the Shriners coming to town with camel rides, becomes a big deal. So too can Maxwell Street Days, free chocolate milk during Dairy Days, Knights of Columbus barbeques, corn mazes, citywide rummage sales, tractor pulling competitions, melon raids, and homecoming bonfires.   You just do the best you can for entertainment. When necessary, there's always that possibility of resorting to annual lutefisk feeds, occasional snipe hunts, cow chip throwing contests, mutton busting, ice shanty pageants, demolition derbies, or catfish noodling.   And of course, if all else fails, there is always Eucjre in the cards.

Weather can be eventful as well. No hometown folklore would be complete without recollecting the storm of the century when granny's home floated downstream, a blizzard which shut down everything, for a week, or the sudden deep freeze that left farmer Jones prized Holstein frozen upright and caused the remaining herd to produce ice cream instead of milk. As for myself, I will never forget the horrific tornado that darn near carried away an entire neighboring town.

LOST TRADES: The rise and fall of any community is usually linked to specific industries. Lumbering and mining dominated many. When the resources dwindled, a community's ability to replace such losses, became a do or die situation. In my hometown, one of the biggest surprises for me was a once flourishing cigar industry, formerly house in what eventually became the Ben Franklin Store. However, long lost are the ma and pa operations, the individual tradesmen, and storekeepers who represented the area's lifeblood. Just west of here, there even use to be a thriving button-making industry, supplied by the river rats who harvested clam shells.

In years past, it's likely your hometown region included cobblers, blacksmiths, harness makers, farriers, wheelwrights, sawyers, millers, lamplighters, cheese-makers, haberdashers, seamstresses, soda jerks, ice cutters, milkmen, paper route cyclists, bootleggers, stumpgrubbers, and grub cooks of the local greasy spoons. Bygone as well are the fuddy-duddy barbershops, where appointments were unheard of and waiting your turn was gladly endured, so as to catch up on the latest gossip. Might be the women folk had similar experiences at their beauty salons.

THE GENERALS: Now replaced by corporate discount chains, general stores were the main street centers of activity and chin wagging. As merchandisers, they were the forerunners to places like S.S. Kresge's, F. W. Woolworth's, Gamble's, Coast to Coast, and Ben Franklin. These in turn have now fallen prey to the superstores. The owners and operators of homegrown general

stores often played a major role in local politics and sponsored many local sports teams. As prosperous merchants, these proprietors built some of the towns' most aristocratic mansions.

ROOM & BOARD: Chances are, near the edge of the business district in your hometown, is an ancient elder who desperately needs physical therapy. This place represents the town's original hotel. If it is anything like the one in my hometown, this aging codger has been forever filled with a whole bunch of geezers. Many of these hotels formerly served as stagecoach and Greyhound bus stops. While elegant in their heydays, the accumulated years of these once-grand plazas have now turned them into old folks' homes. Though some have been restored and rehabbed, far too many have not. As for the one in my hometown, I was never brave enough to venture past the front counter and thus cannot share much about its mysterious interior. However, my friends and I certainly came to know the vintage characters who resided within.

GAS SSED UP: Because Grampy Sully operated one of the first gas stations in my hometown, I amquite partial to the role represented by these petro places. Though small in size, this town of mine boasted a Cities Service, DX, Skelly, Shell, Mobil, Texaco, and two Standard Oil stations. Perhaps I missed naming one or two. Whenever traveling to bigger cities, I always resented that my hometown did not have one of those cool Sinclair Gas Stations with the rooftop dinosaur. There cannot be any complaining on my part however. Sully's Cities Service station kept me well-supplied with NFL bottle cap and Sugar Daddy collectors' cards, along with empty White Owl and Dutch Masters cigar boxes in which to store them.

Having spent endless hours sitting atop the Firestones lined up next to Grampy's desk, to this day, I still become nostalgic over the smell of new tires. At times, I recall my fingers numbed by far too many dips into the icy water of his genuine Coca Cola cooler. Then there was that time that should be forgotten, when Grampy sternly scolded me for attempting to joyride on the hydraulic lift. Then again, any tongue-lashing from Grampy Sully paled in comparison to a gruff encounter with Grandpa Tom. It was always better to get caught goofing off at the gas station rather than down on the farm. Without a doubt, your hometown has gas station memories as well.

FAITHFUL FRATERNALS: When it comes to the folklore of civic pride and compassion, it often starts at the local American Legion hall, VFW clubhouse, Masonic Temple, or Elks, Moose, and Eagles lodges. In many hometowns, these become the major gathering places for special events, fundraisers, and memorials. The heyday of such benefactors has long since passed. Still, along with their auxiliaries, these charitable organizations continue to make a hometown difference. That elk atop the downtown lodge and cannon fronting the American Legion building, are constant reminders of good deeds and a close-knit community. Still, the Masonic Lodge's recent bake sale of Cornish pasties with jalapeno, seems to me like the equivalent of putting ketchup on lefse.

A SONG & DANCE: Many hometowns were once much more cultured than you ever thought possible. In years past, it was not unusual for even a small town to house an Opera House. This term often applied to both theaters and auditoriums where musicals, dramas, concerts, and ballroom galas were staged. Unfortunately, during the Depression Era these sites became inactive as entertainment centers and eventually converted to stores, repair shops, and storage buildings.

RIDING THE RAILS: Any community touched by a rail system had landmarks that may now be gone and forgotten. While some towns have managed to preserve their old depots, chances are that yours may be forever lost. Perhaps your town even had multiple depots based on the different rail systems that crisscrossed through it.

The existence of railroads also meant two peripheral additions. Referred to as "hobo jungles", most rail yards had gathering spots for the meandering transients. For those of more material means, roadhouses sprung up near most depots. These were by no stretch of the imagination, elegant establishments. Many became temporary residences for migrant workers or flop houses for the hopelessly overindulged.

What continues to intrigue me is the skeleton train, marooned next to H-78 in the neighboring county. Along an abandoned section of rail line, nearly one hundred boxcars sit eerily on the tracks. As if picked clean by vultures, all that remains are the rusting metal wheels and frames. It appears to be the iron horse equivalent to the fabled elephant's graveyard.

SCHOOL DAZE: Legendary teachers and pranks define every school. Just when I thought that my parochial educators were the most formidable on earth, my dad then told me of his fifth grade public school teacher, who wielded a thick section of rubber hose and caused one student to jump out the classroom window while escaping punishment. As for any fabled pranks, be careful not to reveal any ideas for the future generations. No school folklore would be complete without also including your grandpa's recollections of trudging five miles to classes during the most horrendous snowstorms.

POP CULTURE: Generally located within the drug stores of many towns, soda fountains served also as cultural centers. Having two drug stores in my hometown created a dividing line. While it was the young twerps who were relegated to the corner drug Store, just down the street was another reserved for the older and much cooler crowd. Of course, those with wheels, high- tailed it instead, out to Merle's A&W. By no means have the McDonald's, Burger King's, or Taco Bell's of today, replaced the character of these disappearing dynasties. Towns where soda fountains continue to operate are blessed with nostalgic good fortune

THE BIJOUS: Hometown theaters, with their gothic facades and illuminated marquees, continue to grace the main streets of small town America. However, their past role as more than simply movie houses seems forgotten. Many represented the community's only exposure to vaudeville comedians, burlesque dancers, singers, actors, orators, and political campaigners. My dad recalled the day when a highfalutin architect named Frank demanded him to sit elsewhere, so as to occupy the most central seat in our local theater. The celebrities who once set the stage in your hometown may astound you.

Sometimes it is the theater owners who are just as entertaining. During my first years of attending our downtown theater, standing sentry at the interior door stood the stony-faced manager, whose stare silently roared to everyone passing through, "Don't ever mess with me or mess around in my theater". Years later when the new owner took over, it was learned that his name was "Otto". This comical sounding name became fair game for all us juveniles. Once the movie began, it became inevitable that someone would soon shout out "Otto, Otto". On the other side of the theater, a chant would echo back "Otto, Otto". If for some reason this was not harassing enough, an empty Jawbreakers box would be blown through to create obnoxious quacking noises. Like clockwork, Otto responded by charging down the aisle while flailing his flashlight and attempting to spotlight the culprits. That Otto could sure put on a show.

FAIR MINDED: While most towns wish they had their own fairgrounds, rivalries among neighboring communities oftentimes dictated the outcome. Although my hometown once had fairgrounds, located at the site of the north side feed mill, it was politically traded off to a nearby town in exchange for housing the county courthouse. As such, one town got year round law and order while the other reveled in a week long 4-h festivities.

Going back to the late 1800's, area fairs hosted more than just pleasantries. Sponsored bare-knuckle fights attracted crowds of gawkers and the home region's contending brawler. . These fights were not only rewarded prize money, yet also community bragging rights. Wrestling matches were popular as well, which around here, featured a local favorite known as "Strangler Lewis".

SIDE POCKETS & GUTTERS: Although local pool halls can become bastions for old fogies with stogies, they actually serve as much more. For my friends and I, Kelly's Pool Hall was the only place we had to hang out. Having two wraparound counters, the front one provided soft drinks, while the other furnished just the opposite. Toward the back was the smoke filled billiards arena, reserved for adults only. The one in-town bowling alley at this time, sat housed in an underground bunker, just beneath my dad's auto parts store. In order to bowl, someone in our group had to volunteer to perch precariously behind the pin-setting machine and reload the bowling pins. Located two miles south of town was a more modern and expansive bowling center called Midway. Of course, getting there required either hitchhiking or begging for a ride from an older sibling. Once there, then meant t contending with the tough kids from the nearby rival town.

ON A ROLL: As hard as it may be to imagine, there was a boom era in roller-skating. This resulted in many towns hosting a wooden-floored arena, frequented by both young and old. These later became stores, dance halls, and storage buildings.

When the roller-skating craze faded, kids in my hometown began dismantling skates and attaching the wheels to 2' x 4' boards. These makeshift skateboards had narrow wheelbases and an unstable nature, thus leading to multiple knee and elbow injuries. When commercial skateboards first became available, I convinced Grammy Agnes to buy me one for my birthday. Accompanied by her to the toy store, I selected a blue-striped skateboard from the bin full of them. Grammy then looked at me and asked why I was not getting one for each foot. Just imagine what a fete for both feet that would be.

BRANCHING OUT:. Darn near extinct nowadays, the fortified enclaves perched among branches, have become few and far between. Most city slickers cannot relate to them, yet tree forts were once a trademark of small towns. The beastly mansion had two in its backyard. The better one, nestled atop a huge walnut tree, got eliminated by the utility company when it ran new lines to the next door neighbors. Constructed in a box elder, the second one was often infested by the nasty bugs associated with this tree. When I began building a tree fort in Grandpa Tom's cherished apple tree, the endeavor did not go over well with this patriarch. Due to modern landscaping and manicured lawns, tree fort craftsmanship has become a lost art.

WATERRED DOWN: Never let your community spirit become dampened by the glumness of the local waterworks. If your town is fortunate enough, it has something out of the ordinary rather than that typical golf ball profile atop a giant tee. In my hometown, our water tower resembled a lofty structure of medieval masonry. One could easily imagine a damsel-in-distress being held captive within. However, an enlightened engineer decided that it was certain to become a Leaning Tower of Pisa and eventually topple upon its neighbors. As such, it has now been vanquished. Perhaps that indigenous old titan in your neck of the woods continues to stand tall.

WHATEVER AILS YOU: Nothing speaks folklore like home remedies. With Grandma SeCelia, it was blood-red mercurochrome for cuts; udder balm for sores and abrasions; mouth wash for stinging nettles; and a mixture of milk and baking soda for bee stings. Grammy Agnes insisted on blackberry brandy for lower intestinal problems. As for my mom, Esther, I'm still not sure why she made me swallow that awful cod liver oil. They each recommended a thorough soaping for foul language. And of course, some folks still abide to a claim that oiling the chassis with distilled spirits, resolves most nagging pains.

THE SEEDY SIDE: Some may not wish to admit it, yet three age-old trades served many a community. During the Prohibition era, there is a good chance that your local hotel harbored a backroom speakeasy. Odds are, it was also furnished by a well-known bootlegger. This is where the reliable gossip comes in. You will need to coerce your local old timers to uncover this information. Perhaps, you'll need to do the same and even more vigorously, to discern anything about the long-ago resident brothels. Do not be surprised if this line of inquiry meets with resistance and denial. Adding to the bad habits, gambling joints also took their chances in a lot of small towns.

GRAVEST SITES: Here is where secrets lie buried. To truly learn the heritage, ethnicity, and religious convictions of a community, you must visit its cemeteries. While stepping carefully, you may also need to step further. Many towns have graveyards separated by affiliation and nationality. A few are even dislocated due to the cause of death, like epidemics or historic battles. Obscured within my hometown is a cholera cemetery. Several miles south of town, alongside a dusty gravel road, is the forlorn grave-marker of the first territorial governor. Some say it is only a marker with no grave beneath it. Just west of town is a Manx burial ground, reserved for those who immigrated from the Isle of Mann. Most country churches around here include adjacent plots where members of past congregations lie interned. Throughout each and every cemetery, the tombstones themselves have stories to tell. Visitors to these sacred sites, such as local mediums and Halloween hooligans, oftentimes become storied as well.

SEEKING ASYLUM: Perhaps some hometowns do not want to admit it, yet oftentimes just beyond the village boundaries is a reclusive building that towers in the middle of nowhere. Originally termed asylums, these places later became known as the county funny farms or old folk's homes. Nowadays, most have been converted to modern nursing facilities. However, in their early days, they served as isolated enclaves for mental illness, tuberculosis, and other maladies scorned by the public. My dad's postcard collection showcases numerous photos relating to the asylum outside our hometown. However, what once transpired within this institution remains a mystery of sorts. Possibly, your hometown borders on a similar mystery.

JUNK GALORE: Do not dump the idea of looking into your hometown's garbage. Junkyards say a lot about where you are from. Before the advent of ecological landfills, many towns hosted elaborate depositories, while others simply relied on any gully near the outskirts. To the north of my hometown, there were several communities where the trash troves became entertainment centers. Tourists would gather at sunset to watch the black bears emerge and sift through the garbage. It was quite the wild and wooly scene. In your search, do not fail to uncover those home-based hoarders as well. Every town has at least one Junkyard George.

OUTDOOR LIFE: Forget finding these anymore. Every community once had them, yet they are now long gone. Demised by both decay and juvenile delinquency, there disappearances lend themselves to varying hometown tales. Knocked over as pranks, burned atop homecoming bonfires, or simply transferred to the lawn of the school principal, their uses were as innovative as the hometown citizenry demanded.

DEEP ROOTED: Most folks think of root cellars as dank and earthy areas beneath old houses. You may be surprised to learn however, that some old homesteads, like that of my Grampy Sully, had backyard root cellars. Sealed off and planted over years ago, imagine what you might find by digging one up. That is what my friend did as he discovered buried treasures.

IN THE SPIRIT: For the sake of community spirit, many hometowns have a resident ghost. Tracing the twisted roots of these phantoms can be an enlightening experience. The early stories about ghosts were often instigated by reports from traveling salesmen and local doctors on nighttime house calls. During the late 1800's and well into the 20th century, séances, exorcisms, witch hunts, snake oil sales, and other occult practices were commonplace and even fashionable. In the town where I received my university degree, there was a times past institution known as the "Spook College", where occult practices, alchemy, and other mysterious ways could be learned. Just east of my hometown, a Wiccan congregation resides in the neighboring village. Every place is bestowed with haunts and haunting. It is more than likely that your hometown has had its bewitching moments.

It continues to fascinate me, that my hometown is riddled with creepy underground tunnels. Once the mineral resources were depleted, these mine shafts were sealed off. Left within were the ore carts, carbide lanterns, pick axes, and according to some accounts, even the mules. Old timers claim that if you put your ear to the ground on a quiet night, the mules can still be heard braying in the catacombs below.

CLANDESTINE CRITTERS: Along with stories of resident ghosts, most places have their share of mysterious critters. Although those werewolf, Bigfoot, and swamp creature sightings challenge the imagination, the chances of giant serpents, wild beasts, and other oddball animals have an actual basis. In my hometown, the stories still continue about a cougar on the loose. North of here, the feral pigs which fiendishly morphed into tusk-enamored monsters, are all too real. A white wolf chained to a classic car is definitely a possibility. So too is a red kangaroo in the nearby countryside. However, the more each tale ages, the more embellished it becomes. That is just the beauty of folklore.

FOOD FOR THOUGHT: To discover the folklore of any region, just taste it. Based on the amount of cheese curds and brats consumed by me, there's no guesswork as to where I am from. Hereabouts, pasties are also a big deal. My Aunt Hazel became renowned for baking these Cornish meat pies. The lefse and flat bread made by Grandma SeCeliar were second to none. Fortunately, she shied away from preparing lye-soaked lutefisk, a Scandinavian dish for those lacking any sense of smell or taste. However, Grandpa Tom could never be deterred from chewing on pickled herring.

Head east of here and you'll eventually find a bakery filled with Polish paczkis, Danish kringles, or giant cream puffs. At last year's state fair, over a quarter million cream puffs were devoured. I've attended a few wedding sin this part of the state, where they serve up wildcat, a high grade hamburger eaten raw. No, I did not have the nerve to sample this delicacy. By the way, if Rocky Mountain oysters pickled pigs' feet, or cow tongues are on the menu, please do not invite me. The same goes for blood sausage, deer hearts, and limburger cheese. To show that I am not all that persnickety, I'll gladly accept a monkeytail, deep-fried Oreo, elephant ear, or Dutch pannekoek. Above all, none compare to mom's sugar cookies.

The local yokels, who bear hunt up north, rave about their bruin burgers. Then again, these same guys savor smoked carp, eelpout, and sturgeon steaks. One former staple use to be known as side pork, although I am not sure it even exists anymore. Younger brother Tom claims that walleye cheeks are absolutely the best. My choice would be a juicy chuck roast with onions and fried potatoes, preferably, one not representing a stumpgrubber's oven-baked woodchuck.

IN THE CARDS: As for my hometown, you can easily tell the locals from the outsiders. The native sons and daughters play Euchre, Dirty Clubs, and sometimes an occasional game of Cribbage. Those newcomers from the east side of the state keep trying to infiltrate with Sheepshead. The real foreigners expose themselves by showcasing Pinnacle and Rummy Royal. A few old timers still hang on with Bridge. For a short while,

Hearts began to catch on, until the Euchre players again came to their senses. The hardcore enthusiasts now play six-handed. However, I am not sure why my friends up north remain addicted to Scum and Duckett. Perhaps they would be much better off by switching over to Grandma SeCelia's cherished standard of Starve to Death

WELL SEASONED: In this neck of the woods, we do not need a Farmer's Almanac to predict the weather. Robins signal the arrival of spring. Mosquitoes make it a point that summer is upon us. Southbound geese send a message that fall is in session. As for winter, it officially begins and ends whenever a fisherman's truck plunges through thin ice. There are other predictors as well. The start of the state boys' basketball tournament usually guarantees a blizzard of heavy wet snow. Just when the campsites fill up on Memorial Day weekend, a cold front with rain is almost sure to set in. Even the mildest of summers turns to blistering heat and wretched humidity whenever the county fair begins. A wagon load of pumpkins at the edge of town indicates that Halloween spookily approaches and deer season is not far away. The same goes for the local corn mazes.

There are a number of use-to-be indicators that have weathered away. Kids no longer post "Nightcrawlers for Sale" signs throughout trout season. The maple syrup enclaves known as the sugarbush, no longer dot this area with their bucket brigades. The mid-summer sweet corn wagons at every busy intersection have dwindled down to just a couple. Giant igloos of hay have replaced the rectangular bales which stacked so perfectly during the first and second crops of alfalfa season. Far and few between are the snow fences that once barricaded both the town and countryside. And the dead deer hanging from the neighbors' trees and angled ladders just ain't what they use-to-be at Thanksgiving time.

NAME GAME: Nowhere in this book will you come across the modern day name of my hometown. There are more than enough clues however, to reveal its' true identity. Like many communities which now are elders, these places have changed names over time. My hometown had three former names. Oftentimes this occurred because opposite ends of town had different labels. Eventually the names were traded off for the solo moniker now withstanding. Retracing a nearly-forgotten name like Dirty Hollow, can uncover and untangle more folklore than ever expected.

HAPPY ENDINGS: Regardless of where your search takes you, expect the unexpected. Do not be afraid to uncover the hidden treasures within your hometown. Be careful at this juncture, for there is always a reason why some treasures have remained hidden. And most of all, do not be surprised to learn that there really is no place like home.

Additional information on the author and these stories is available at:

folktattler.com.